"Claudia and I have something to tell you, don't we, my love?"

Adam slid a possessive arm around her waist, his hand warm against her silk-clad flesh, making it tingle with unwanted awareness.

"I know it's early days after the loss of her first husband, but when we met again we realized that what we felt for each other, all those years ago, was still there, and important to us. So we plan to marry just as soon as it can be arranged and we hope, sir, that you will understand, give us your blessing and be happy for us."

Claudia felt her father's questioning eyes on her and flinched. The silence wrapped her like a shroud. She shivered with tension. What could she possibly do or say? Adam's bombshell had left her shell-shocked.

DIANA HAMILTON is a true romantic and fell in love with her husband at first sight. They still live in the fairy-tale Tudor house where they raised their three children. Now the idyll is shared with eight rescued cats and a puppy. But despite an often chaotic life-style, ever since she learned to read and write Diana has had her nose in a book—either reading or writing one— and plans to go on doing just that for a very long time to come.

Books by Diana Hamilton

HARLEQUIN PRESENTS®
1896—IN NAME ONLY
1920—A GUILTY AFFAIR
1936—SCANDALOUS BRIDE
1956—THE MILLIONAIRE'S BABY

DIANA HAMILTON

A Husband's Price

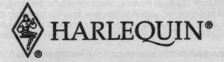

TORONTO • NEW YORK • LONDON
AMSTERDAM • PARIS • SYDNEY • HAMBURG
STOCKHOLM • ATHENS • TOKYO • MILAN • MADRID
PRAGUE • WARSAW • BUDAPEST • AUCKLAND

ISBN 0-373-11998-4

A HUSBAND'S PRICE

First North American Publication 1998.

Copyright © 1998 by Diana Hamilton.

CHAPTER ONE

CLAUDIA passed an uncertain hand over the photograph album. She hadn't looked at it in years; hadn't wanted to set eyes on it even. She tried to walk away and out of the room but somehow couldn't, then, her teeth biting into the warm flesh of her full lower lip, she gave into temptation and knew she'd regret it.

Sitting abruptly at the table beneath the library's stone mullioned window, she hooked a strand of soft brown, deadly straight, shoulder-length hair behind one ear and tentatively opened the album. Here they all were. All the people; all the memories. All the shattered dreams and broken trust.

Her fingertips shakily grazed the glossy surface of the prints. She had put the album away on the top shelf out of sight a long time ago. Her father must have glanced through it then abandoned it here on the library table. Had he, in his grief, been searching for that lost summer, desperately straining to catch an echo of vanished, happier times?

And here he was. Guy Sullivan, her father. Six years ago, he would have been fifty-two, a big man, in his prime then, his arm around his blonde and beautiful bride of three months. Her stepmother, Helen.

Twenty years her father's junior, recently divorced, the sizzling blonde could have turned into the stepmother from hell, but hadn't. From the day Helen had applied for the position as a relief receptionist here at Farthings Hall, Claudia had seen how attracted her father was. Guy Sullivan had been a widower for eight years, Claudia's mother dying of a rare viral infection when her only child was ten years old.

Three months after their first meeting, Guy and Helen had married. Claudia had been happy for them both; her initial fears that Helen might resent her, or that she might resent the woman who had taken her mother's place in her father's affections, had been unfounded. Helen couldn't have tried harder to charm her new stepdaughter.

And here she herself was: the Claudia of six years ago. Hair much longer then—almost reaching down to her waist—her curves lusher, her smile wide, open, untouched in those long-gone innocent days by the betrayal that was to come later.

Her eyes misted as she looked at the photograph. She'd been eighteen years old and happy to be spending the summer at home before going to teacher training college. She'd been glad to help out around Farthings Hall, the exclusive country house hotel and restaurant that was both home and livelihood not only for her father now, but for his father before him.

And there in the background, prophetically perhaps, Tony Favel had been caught by the camera leaning against the stone parapet that bordered the terrace that ran along the west façade of the wonderful old Tudor house.

Tony Favel, her father's accountant, the man who had brought Helen into their lives, introducing her as some kind of distant cousin, keen to make a new life for herself after a messy divorce. Even now she could hear the echo of his following words. 'And haven't you said, Guy, you're looking for a part-time receptionist for when Sandy packs it in to have that baby she's expecting?'

Tony Favel. At the time the photograph had been taken, he would have been thirty. Even then, his lint-blond hair was beginning to recede, his waistline to thicken. Claudia swallowed hard, her vivid blue eyes clouding as they rested on the grainy, slightly out-of-focus image of her husband. Tony Favel, whom she had married at the end of that summer six years ago.

Slowly, not wanting to, yet driven by something too dark for her to understand, Claudia turned the page and found what she had known she would find. And feared. All those pictures of Adam.

At the end of that summer, she'd vowed to destroy every last one of them, to rip them to shreds and burn them. But, when it had come down to it, she hadn't been able to bring herself to touch them. Or, at least, that was what she had told herself at the time. Love and hate: different sides of the same coin. She had told herself she hated him but obviously she must have still been in love with him. Why else would she have found it impossible to destroy his likenesses?

She had taken all but one of the photographs of Adam herself and, looking at them now, she couldn't deny that fatal male beauty. Or deny that those smoky grey eyes, that rumpled, over-long black hair, those pagan-god good looks and body to match hid a black, black heart.

The odd picture out was the one of her and Adam together. Adam's arm was placed possessively around her waist, pulling her close into the side of his lithely powerful body, and she was gazing adoringly up into his face. So there they were, the two of them, eternally smiling, caught for posterity looking as if they were walking confidently through the best, the most blissfully happy, the most wonderful summer of their lives...

She never looked back into the past because it hurt too much, but now she couldn't seem to help herself and the memories came crowding in. She could clearly see her younger self running lightly down the service stairs on that sunny, early summer day six years ago.

She'd spent the best part of the morning helping the housekeeper, Amy, to ready the guest suites. There were only four of them; by country house hotel standards Farthings Hall was small. But very, very exclusive. There was a waiting list as long as your arm both for accommodation and for the restaurant tables.

And, after all that hoovering, polishing and dusting, she'd been good and ready for a dose of that glorious sunshine she'd only so far yearned for through the spotless, glittering upstairs windows. She'd been just eighteen years old, was at the very beginning of the long summer holiday, had done her duty by helping Amy and now smelt freedom.

'Oops!' She skidded to an abrupt halt before she knocked her new stepmother to kingdom come. 'Sorry—didn't see you!'

Small and willowy with hair like spun sunlight, Helen always made Claudia feel large and clumsy and, just recently, awkward and a bit in the way. Oh, Helen had never, ever, given her an unkind word or look either before her marriage to Guy or after, but for the past few days there'd been an edginess about her, a brittleness that went hand in hand with discontent.

But thankfully not today. Claudia felt her muscles relax as Helen's narrow green eyes gleamed at her. 'Such energy! Oh, to be young and full of bounce again!'

'You're not old.' Claudia grinned, falling in step beside her stepmother who was heading down the passage to the courtyard entrance. At eighteen, just, she regarded the thirties—even the early thirties as she knew Helen to be—as knocking on the door of middle age. But there was something timeless about Helen's sexy little body, golden hair and perfect features.

'Thanks.' Helen's voice was dry. She reached the door first and pushed it open. The sunlight streamed through and made her a dazzling, glittering figure in her lemon-yellow sheath dress and all that chunky gold jewellery she seemed to favour. 'Coming?'

Claudia had promised herself a walk to the rocky little cove that could only be reached via the deep valley that bisected the Hall's extensive grounds, but if Helen wanted her company she would gladly tag along. She usually fell in with other people's wishes because she liked those around her to be happy and, perhaps just as importantly, she liked people to be pleased with her.

Like a big, exuberant puppy, she thought with wry, self-mocking humour. She could almost hear herself panting, feel her tongue hanging out!

'Sure. Where to?'

'To find Old Ron. He hasn't sent the fruit and veg up to the kitchens yet. Chef's furious. Lunches will be starting in an hour. I said I'd chase him up. Besides—' green eyes gleamed up into the speedwell-blue of Claudia's '—Guy hired a dogsbody to help Ron through the summer.' Her sudden giggle was infectious. 'He may be some kind of a drop-out of no fixed abode, but he sure is gorgeous! Worth the trek down to the kitchen gardens any time of the day!' She paused significantly. 'Or night!'

Claudia giggled right back. She knew Helen didn't mean it; she had been married only for a couple of months or so, and she wouldn't have eyes for any other man. 'I didn't know Dad had been hiring,' she commented, striding along the raked gravel path.

She wasn't surprised that this was the first she'd heard of a new employee. Recently she'd overheard her father and his new wife tersely arguing over Helen's apparently sudden decision to give up her post. She had seemed to be saying that now she was married to the owner she shouldn't have to work like a hired skivvy—though she would be happy to continue to do the flowers. Claudia had kept well out of the way of both of them, waiting until they'd sorted out their differences. She could imagine only one thing more embarrassing than overhearing them squabbling and that would be overhearing them making love.

Firmly squashing that thought, she asked, 'So when did Adonis join the crew? Is he really a homeless drop-out?' Claudia knew she was very lucky to have somewhere like Farthings Hall to call home. She couldn't imagine what it would be like to have no-where.

Helen shrugged slim, lightly tanned shoulders. 'Goodness knows. He turned up on a clapped-out old motorbike a couple of days ago, looking for work. He admitted he was "just drifting" and apparently seemed happy enough to have the use of that old cara-van at the back of the glasshouses for the summer, plus his food and pin money, in exchange for helping Old Rob around the grounds. His name's Adam, by the way. Adam Weston.'

But Claudia wasn't really listening as she followed Helen through into the walled kitchen garden, her thoughts exclusively for Old Ron now. The ancient groundsman couldn't cope. Everyone knew it except him, which was obviously why her father had decided to hire someone to help out for the summer. How would Old Ron feel when he had to make way per-manently for someone fit and young, someone who could actually walk faster than a snail?

Old Ron had worked here forever. Her grandfather had hired him initially, before Farthings Hall had been converted into the now exclusive country house hotel with what was reputed to be the best restaurant in Cornwall. He'd been here ever since, never marrying, inhabiting a flat conversion above the old stable block. Of course, Dad would never ask him to vacate his home, or pay rent, and, knowing her father, he would probably find him a token something or other to do, just so the old man wouldn't feel entirely useless...

Then, for the second time in thirty minutes, Claudia almost ran her stepmother down. Helen had stopped without warning in the centre of the path, just inside the arched doorway in the high, ivy-clad, red-brick wall—the heated summer air was suddenly and unexpectedly thrumming with a tension so sharply intense that Claudia found herself instinctively holding her breath.

She expelled it slowly when she saw what Helen was staring at, her stepmother's green eyes laughing, maybe even teasing just a little.

The new hired help was enough to bring a smile of glowing pleasure to any woman's eyes.

Adam Weston was just as magnificent as Helen had implied, only more so. Leaning against a garden fork, dressed only in frayed denim cut-offs and scuffed working boots, he blew Claudia's mind.

The breadth of his rangy shoulders was, she admitted admiringly, deeply impressive, accentuating the narrowness of his hips, the length of his leanly muscular legs. The tan of his skin was slicked with sweat and his forehead, beneath the soft fall of rumpled dark hair, was beaded with it. And his eyes, an intriguing smoky grey, narrowed now in overt male appraisal, were firmly fixed on the slender, golden figure of her stepmother.

Claudia shivered. It was a brilliant day, the hottest this summer so far. Yet she shivered right down to the soles of her grungy canvas shoes. She stepped forward, out of the shadows, uselessly regretting her faded, a-bit-baggy old jeans, the washed-out old shirt she wore for house-cleaning.

Her movement broke the spell. Whatever had been here, shimmering and stinging in the scented summer air, had gone. Helen said, her musical voice low and quite definitely husky, 'Adam, meet your employer's solitary offspring and pride of his life—Claudia. Dearest, say hello to Adam. And then, perhaps, he can run along and find Old Ron before Chef arrives with his cleaver!'

'Hi there—' Adam Weston brushed the wayward hank of soft dark hair out of his eyes and stepped forward, extending a strong, long-boned hand. And smiled.

And Claudia, for the first, and very probably the last, time in her life, fell deeply, shatteringly and quite, quite helplessly in love...

'So there you are.' The mesmeric spell of the past was broken as Guy Sullivan walked slowly into the book-lined room leaning on his ebony-handled cane, a little of the strain leaving his eyes when he saw his daughter. 'Amy's just got back from collecting Rosie from school. They were looking for you.' His eyes fell on the album and he shook his head slightly, admitting, 'I can't think why I wanted to look at that. No good looking into the past—you can't bring it back. Neither of us can.'

Claudia got to her feet and resolutely stuffed the album back in its former hiding place, aware of her father's eyes on her, the rough compassion in his voice. Six weeks ago, his wife and her husband had been killed when the car they were in was mown down on a blind bend on a steep hill by an articulated lorry that had lost its brakes.

Just over a week later, they had discovered that Helen and Tony had been lovers. Their affair had been on and off, but mostly on, since before Tony had introduced the glamorous divorcée and suggested that Guy consider her for the post of relief receptionist.

Her father had made that discovery when he had been going through his dead wife's effects and had happened across diaries and some highly explicit love letters. It had devastated him. Coming on top of the shock of the fatal accident, it had brought about his third heart attack in six years.

It hadn't been anything like as severe as the one he'd had, right out of the blue, at the end of the summer six years ago but, nevertheless, it had weakened him still further and it would be a long time before she could stop worrying about him.

And how she was going to be able to break the other piece of shattering news she couldn't imagine. The thought of what it could do to him terrified her.

'Did you mention the possibility of the loan we need to refurbish the guest suites?' Guy sat on the chair Claudia had vacated and leaned his cane against the table.

His once strong features were now gaunt and grey and Claudia would have done anything to spare him from this final horror. But the best she could do was prevaricate, just for now, delay the inevitable for as long as she possibly could.

Ask the bank manager for a loan? As if!

Her discussion with the manager this afternoon had been on a different topic entirely. Their business was as good as bankrupt, their financial difficulties severe—so severe that selling up was the only option. It was something her father was going to have to be told about. But not now.

Now she asked, changing the subject, 'Where's Rosie?' As a rule she collected her small daughter from school every day, but because of her appointment at the bank she'd had to ask Amy to do it. She didn't know what they would do without the grey-haired, rosy-cheeked dumpling who had been at Farthings Hall as long as Claudia could remember. Amy had done her best to do what she could to fill the gap when Claudia, as a ten-year-old, had been left motherless.

'Amy took her through to the kitchens for some juice. Oh, I forgot to mention it, but Jenny can't come in this evening—summer flu, or some such excuse.' Guy Sullivan got slowly to his feet. 'Look, I can help Amy out round the kitchens—we can take the trickier stuff off the menu—and free you up to take Jenny's place, wait on tables.'

'No, Dad.' Claudia automatically declined the offer. Her father was physically and emotionally frail, and still in need of all the rest he could get. 'Amy and I can manage.'

Ever since Tony had had a falling-out with Chef six months ago—and Claudia had never got to find out what it had been about—she and Amy, with Jenny's help, had been keeping the restaurant going on a reduced and simplified menu. Tony had been reluctant to hire a replacement chef and now Claudia knew why. Tomorrow she would have to cancel the advertisements for the new and experienced staff she'd decided had to be hired if the hotel and restaurant were to continue. There was no point now. The business, their home, was to be sold over their heads.

'Why don't you sit outside, Dad? It's a glorious day; let's make the most of it.' She almost added, While we can, but managed to stop herself in time. 'I'll fetch Rosie and we'll all have tea on the terrace.'

Ten days later, Amy asked rhetorically, 'I guess you can't have told your father the bad news yet?' She filled a mug with strong black coffee and held it out. 'He looked happy, almost back to his old self, when his friend collected him this morning, so he can't know that his home's about to be sold from over his head.'

'I'm a coward,' Claudia admitted wearily, taking the mug of steaming coffee. 'But every day he gets that little bit stronger. And the stronger he gets, the more able he'll be to cope with yet another blow.'

'And what about you?' Amy demanded. 'The blows fell on your head, too. Your husband died; he'd been playing around with that madam, Helen, his own stepmother-in-law, would you believe? And yes—' her round face went scarlet '—I know we're not supposed to speak ill of the dead—but really! So you've had blows, just the same, so why should you have to carry this other load on your own?'

'Because I haven't had three heart attacks in half a

dozen years and because I didn't love Tony, and Dad adored Helen.' Claudia looked at the mug in her hands, and frowned just slightly. 'I really haven't got time to drink this.'

'Of course you have,' Amy asserted firmly. 'This Hallam man won't be looking under beds for fluff or running his fingers round picture frames looking for dust. You've been running around like a scalded cat ever since you got back from taking Rosie to school. So drink your coffee and try to relax. You've got time for that before you need to get changed. And, no matter what anyone else believed, where you're concerned, nobody can pull the wool over my eyes. Like my own daughter, you are. I knew your marriage to Tony Favel wasn't a love match. When you married him you were still hankering after Adam—and don't pop your eyes at me—I knew how you were feeling when he just upped and disappeared. But, like I said, you and Tony rubbed along; you didn't hate him, so what happened must still have been a dreadful shock.'

Claudia eyed her old friend over the rim of her mug as she sipped the hot liquid. What else did Amy suspect? Know?

She didn't want to think about that. She put her mug down on the work surface, changing the subject. 'How many tables are booked for this evening?'

'All of them.' Amy collected the used mugs and up-ended them in the commercial-size dishwasher. 'I dare say we do have to keep going as best we can so it can be sold as a going concern. But thank heaven we're at the end of the season, that's all I can say.'

Casting her eyes over the spotlessly gleaming

kitchen, Claudia nodded her heartfelt agreement. It was early October now and hotel bookings ceased at the end of September, so they didn't have that aspect to worry about. They didn't do lunches, either—they wouldn't start up again until Easter—but evening meals went on right through the year. So yes, that was something they could give thanks for.

And there were other things, too, she admitted as she lay in the warm bath water ten minutes later. Life wasn't all bad; there were tiny glimmers of good luck if you looked hard enough.

The bank manager wasn't exactly an ogre. He had shown considerable if understated compassion at that meeting she'd had with him ten days ago. After painting his pitch-black picture and explaining that Farthings Hall would have to be sold, and preferably as a going concern, to cover those terrifying debts, he had advised, 'Before you have to advertise the property for sale I suggest you contact the Hallam Group—you've heard of them?'

Claudia had nodded. Who hadn't? No one remotely connected to the hotel and leisure industry could be ignorant of that huge and exclusive outfit.

She'd felt suddenly nauseous. One shock too many, she supposed. The bank manager had used the intercom to ask someone called Joyce to bring through a tray of tea, leaning back in his chair then, steepling his fingers as he had continued—just as if she'd denied any knowledge of the Hallam Group—'Quality hotels and leisure complexes; they don't touch anything that's run-of-the-mill or even marginally second-rate. It's mainly a family-run company, as you probably know, and Harold Hallam was the majority shareholder. He died, oh, it must be a good twelve months ago and rumour has it his heir is about to expand, acquire new properties.'

He had paused when the tea was brought through and poured, then had suggested, 'If you could interest them in Farthings Hall and effect a quick sale, it would be better all round—a quick takeover by the Hallam Group would mean less time for the type of speculation that could agitate your father. I suggest you ask your solicitor to get in touch with them.'

Useful advice, because only yesterday her solicitor had phoned to say that someone from the Hallam Group would be coming out to Farthings Hall to meet her this morning to discuss the possibility of a private sale.

'Don't commit yourself to anything. This new chief executive might be trying to show his board of directors what a smart operator he is. Remember, this will be an exploratory meeting only. The legal people can be brought in after the initial informal discussion between the principles. That's the general idea, I believe.'

That suited Claudia. And what suited her even more was David Ingram's invitation to her father. They were near neighbours, had been friends since boyhood, and David had wanted to know how Guy felt about being picked up the next morning. After lunch, they could have a game of chess.

Claudia had breathed a huge sigh of cowardly relief when her father had accepted the invitation. She could have her meeting with the Hallam man with her father none the wiser. Every day that passed without him having to learn the miserable truth was a bonus.

And Rosie was out of the way, too, safely at school. Had she been at home, she would have wanted to be with her mummy, even though she loved Amy to pieces. Serious conversation with a bubbly, demanding five-and-a-bit-year-old was problematical to say the least.

The trouble was, since the death of her daddy and Steppie—as Helen, her stepgrandmother, had preferred to be called—Rosie had become very clingy. Not that either of them had spent much time with the little girl, and both of them had developed the habit of absenting themselves if Rosie had been ill or just plain tiresome.

Their deaths must have left a hole in the little girl's life; one day they'd been around—in the background, but around—and the next they'd been blown away. But possibly the most traumatic thing had been her beloved grandpa's illness and his subsequent need for lots of rest and quiet. Rosie probably couldn't understand why her grandpa could no longer play those boisterous games she enjoyed or read to her for hours on end.

Claudia sighed and heaved herself out of the bath. The Hallam man would be arriving in half an hour. She couldn't remember if the solicitor had actually said his name. But it would be Mr Hallam. She definitely recalled him saying that her visitor was the deceased Harold Hallam's heir. It would be his son. Her solicitor would surely have said, had the new chief executive gone under a name other than the family one.

And what to wear? A simple grey linen suit with a cream silk blouse. Cool, businesslike, entirely suitable for a young widow.

Her soft brown hair caught back into the nape of her neck with a mock-tortoiseshell clip, and with the merest suggestion of make-up, her mind played truant, sliding back to those photographs she'd been looking at on her return from her traumatic meeting with her bank manager. Particularly, the one of her.

How she had changed. Still five feet seven inches, of course, but she'd lost all those lavish curves. After Rosie's birth she'd fined down but now, since the traumas of the last few weeks, she looked positively scrawny. The Claudia in that old photograph had been a cheerful optimist, with laughing eyes and a beaming, open smile.

The mirror image she scrutinised now was older, wiser, a bit of a cynic with an overlay of composure, a strength of will that practically defied anyone to mess with her. She was through with being anyone's eager little doormat. She was twenty-four years old, the age Adam Weston had been when they'd first met. She looked and felt a great deal older.

And another difference: the woman in the mirror was as good as bankrupt. The girl in the photograph had been quite a considerable heiress.

And therein had lain the attraction, of course.

She remembered with absolute and still painful clarity exactly how, over six years ago now, she had discovered that particular home truth.

Helen had told her. Helen had been sitting on the edge of her bed, clad in brief scarlet satin panties and bra, looking absolutely furious, yet finding compassion as she grabbed Claudia's hand and squeezed it.

'And you know what that slimeball Adam Toerag Weston had the gall to say? I can still hardly believe it! He actually told me not to be miffed because he'd been messing about—as he so chivalrously put it— with you! Miffed—I ask you! As if I'd be interested in a loser like him! As if I'd have some furtive, sleazy affair with a jobless, homeless, penniless layabout when I'm married to a lovely, lovely man like your father! But this is the point, dearest—'

Helen had released her hand with a final squeeze, reached for a scarlet satin robe and wrapped it around her body. 'He actually said that he'd played up to you because you were quite an heiress. You'd agreed to marry him, or so he claimed, and, as his darling daughter's husband, Guy wouldn't object to keeping him in the manner to which he had always wanted to become accustomed—not if he didn't want to alienate his darling daughter. I only hope, dearest, that you haven't let him go too far with you, that you haven't actually fallen for him, or anything stupid like that…'

Claudia had closed her eyes to stop the hurt from showing. She had wanted to scream that it wasn't true, that Adam loved her, loved her for herself, that he didn't care about her father's wealth, Farthings Hall, the land, all that stuff. But she had never lied to herself. And if the evidence of her own eyes hadn't been enough there had been that conversation on the first date they'd ever had.

It hadn't been an accident that had found her in the vicinity of the old caravan at the back of the glass-houses about seven hours after she'd first been introduced to Adam. Or an accident that she had been wearing a pair of very brief shorts and her best sleeveless T-shirt. The crisp white garments had shown off her long and shapely legs and accentuated the honey-gold tan she'd managed to acquire.

Her heart had been fluttering wildly as she'd approached the open caravan door, but she'd told herself not to be stupid. She, as his employer's daughter, had the perfect excuse for being here.

She could hear him moving about, whistling tunelessly beneath his breath, and before she could knock or call out he had appeared in the doorway, still wearing nothing but those threadbare cut-offs, a towel slung over one shoulder. Instead of the heavy working boots, he'd been sporting a pair of beat-up trainers.

'Hello again.' He'd smiled that smile. For several seconds Claudia hadn't been able to speak. She'd felt her face go fiery red and had hoped quite desperately that he'd put it down to the heat, to the sun glinting off the roofs of the glasshouses, boiling down from a cloudless blue sky.

'I...' Agitatedly, she had pulled in a deep, deep breath. A huge mistake. Just looking at him, being on the receiving end of that deeply sexy smile, had made her legs go weak, made her breasts feel hot and full and tingly. And dragging air into her lungs that way had made them push against the soft white cloth of her top, and she'd known he'd noticed because his gaze had dropped, fastened there, right there, his lids heavy, thick dark lashes veiling his expression.

So she had begun again, gabbling now. 'I wondered if you have everything you need? The caravan hasn't been used in ages, not since—'

'It's fine. That nice housekeeper of yours—Amy?—supplied me with a bundle of bed- and bathroom linen, food supplies—and the place is clean, sweet as a nut.'

He had loped down the steps, pulling the van door to behind him. Claudia had swallowed a huge lump of disappointment. She'd hoped he'd invite her inside to see for herself. But what he had said was even better, more than she'd hoped for. 'I'm told there's a path through the valley leading down to a cove. I fancied a swim. Coming?'

Was she ever! She'd gone back to the house to get her swimming costume and met him back at the caravan. And it had been lovely, that walk. They'd talked a lot; well, he had, mostly. She'd asked him questions about himself but he'd skirted them, telling her to talk about herself, but she hadn't been able to; there hadn't been much to say. So it had ended up with him asking questions, making comments.

'This is a fantastic place. Magical. How does it make you feel, knowing it will all be yours one day? Not yet, of course, but some time in the future. Will you keep it on? Does the responsibility worry you? Uneasy lies the head that wears the crown—and all that.'

They'd been sitting in the soft golden sand by then, the sun dipping down towards the sea. He hadn't seemed to need an answer; he could almost have been talking to himself. He'd leaned forward, softly tracing the outline of her mouth with the tip of a forefinger. 'You are very lovely.'

And after that everything else had been simple. He'd gone out of his way to confirm his deductions that the land, the house, the business would all be hers in the fullness of time, and had gone ahead and trapped her with the honey-sweet bait of great sex and her own foolish notions of undying romantic love...

Claudia blinked, shaking her head, annoyed with herself, pushing the unwanted memories away. She couldn't remember now what had made her think back to all of that. Adam. Betrayal. Loss.

She pulled herself together and swiftly left the room, heading down the stairs for the library. She'd asked Amy to bring Mr Hallam there when he arrived at eleven-thirty. Then bring coffee through.

She glanced at her watch and groaned. Eleven thirty-five. He might already be here. Unforgivable of her to have gone off into that backward-looking trance, wasting time.

'He's arrived!' Amy appeared at the foot of the stairs, her voice low and urgent. 'I put him in the library and said you wouldn't be a minute. I was on my way to warn you.'

'Yes, I'm sorry to be late.' Claudia gave Amy a reassuring smile. She should have been there to greet the man, of course, but she was only late by a few minutes, not long enough to warrant Amy's obvious anxiety.

'Wait.' Amy caught her arm before she could hurry through. 'You don't understand. It's not a Mr Hallam, like you said. It's—'

'Remember me?'

The library door now stood open, framing the impressive, immaculately suited figure of Adam Weston.

'Because I remember you.' He moved forward, eyes fixed on Claudia's speechless lips, then they lifted to clash with hers. 'How could I possibly forget?'

He smiled, a sensual movement of that wickedly crafted mouth. It was sexier than ever. But his eyes didn't smile; didn't come near it. 'Might I ask you to bring us some coffee, Amy?' he asked the stunned-seeming housekeeper. 'Mrs Favel and I have a great deal to talk through.'

CHAPTER TWO

SILENCE. Shock clamped Claudia into a small, dark, very tight corner. Clamped her in so tightly she could barely breathe, let alone speak.

How dared he show his face here? Oh, how dared he?

Then the thick silence eased just a little, slowly nudged away by the inevitable impingement of ordinary, everyday sounds. The sonorous, echoey ticking of the longcase clock; the stutter and grumble of machinery from directly outside as Bill, the new groundsman, tried to start the ride-on mower; Amy's voice—the sound of the words she spoke as they fell on the still air, but not the sense of them—and the sound of the housekeeper's feet on the polished wood floor blocks as she walked away; the thump of her own, wild heartbeats.

He'd changed, and yet he hadn't. That was the first coherent thought she had. Though how a thought could be coherent and contradictory was a total mystery.

At thirty, Adam Weston was a spectacularly attractive man. The once over-long, soft black hair was expertly cut and those pagan-god features were tougher now, more forceful than they'd been six years ago. That superbly fit body was clothed in a silky dark grey suit, crafted by a master tailor, instead of the scruffy

27

cut-offs and washed-out T-shirts that had been his habitual wear during that long, hot summer when she had loved him so.

A man with those looks, that kind of honed physique, would always land on his feet, especially if he still possessed that laid-back, lazy charm, the charm that had had her swooning at his feet from that first unforgettable smile.

Obviously, he'd finally married an heiress. Well, bully for him! she thought cynically, wondering if he'd come here to gloat because he'd done very well, thank you, for himself and she was practically bankrupt.

'What do you want, Adam?' Her voice was tight, quaky, like an old woman's. And she knew she didn't look anything like the lushly curvaceous, fresh-faced and dewy-eyed eighteen-year-old he'd sweet-talked into his bed all those years ago. She didn't need that look of distaste he was giving her to tell her that, while he'd been able to bring himself to the point of actually making love to her six years ago, he found her a total turn-off now.

Claudia lifted her chin and told herself she didn't care, in either event. 'I'm expecting someone. Can you see yourself out?'

She knew she sounded like a snob of the first water, the lady of the manor ordering the boot boy out of her rarefied presence, and saw his eyes narrow and harden. Those smoky grey eyes that didn't smile any more.

'You're expecting *me*, Mrs Favel.' His voice was clipped. Hard. As hard as his eyes. 'The Hallam

Group,' he reminded her, as if, Claudia thought resentfully, he thought she was completely stupid.

But hadn't he always thought that? That she had rampaging hormones where other people had brains. That she'd be a pushover, blindly and ecstatically rushing into marriage with a drifter who was only interested in getting his hands on her assets, which, in those days, had been considerable.

Within a few short weeks he'd had her besotted, head over heels in love and so eager to accept his proposal of marriage she'd practically fallen over herself. And the only thing that had stopped her dragging him down the aisle had been the evidence of her own eyes...

Adam walking out of Helen's bedroom, his face tight and furious. He'd been so furious he hadn't seen her at the top of the service stairs, her arms full of freshly laundered bed-linen.

Helen. Helen sitting on the edge of her bed, clad only in those wisps of underwear. Furious, too, spitting out that poison about him only being interested in her, Claudia's future financial prospects, ramming home the final nail in the coffin of her love for him with, 'He must have seen me come up here—he knows your father's out. I was getting ready to have a shower before changing. He just walked in and started on about the way he'd always fancied me. He said we could have fun—adult fun. He was sick of playing with a child, only the child, as it happened, would one day come into a fortune. He meant you, my poor sweet! And then...heaven help me...I told him to pack his bags and get off Farthings Hall property. I said if he was still around when your father got back he'd regret it.'

'I was told to expect the late Mr Hallam's heir,' she said now, her voice stiff with remembered outrage and pain. Then added insultingly, 'Not the tea boy.'

His smile was wintry. 'And I always thought you had such lovely manners.' He turned, walked away, moving over the huge, raftered hall back towards the library. 'Harold Hallam was my mother's brother. He didn't marry and, as far as anyone knows, he had no issue. I inherited his holding in the Group. Perhaps now we might begin our discussions, provided you're satisfied with my credentials. Unless, of course, you're no longer interested in any offer my company might be prepared to come up with.'

Disorientated, Claudia stared at his retreating back. Such wide, spare shoulders tapering down to that narrow, flat waist, such long, long legs, and all of him so elegantly packaged in a suit so beautifully cut it could only have come from Savile Row.

'So you finally fell on your feet.' She truly hadn't realised she'd spoken the thought aloud until he turned at the door to the library, grey eyes chilling, that utterly sensual, boldly defined mouth contemptuous.

'So it would seem.'

She tilted her chin in challenging defiance, her blue eyes cool. After what he'd done to her, did he really expect to make her feel ashamed of her lack of manners? Did he seriously expect her to apologise?

It would give her enormous satisfaction to ask him to leave.

But he'd disappeared into the library—as if he already owned the place—and she pulled in a deep breath, drew back her shoulders and followed.

She found Amy practically on her heels, the delicate china coffee cups rattling companionably on the tray she carried.

Claudia stepped aside at the doorway to allow the housekeeper passage, wincing as the older woman put the tray down on the long, polished table, a huge smile splitting her rosy face as she marvelled, 'Well, and isn't this a turn up for the books, young Adam? Who'd have thought—?'

'Thank you, Amy,' Claudia interrupted smoothly. Amy had had a soft spot for the young Adam Weston all those years ago, making sure he was lavishly supplied from the kitchens, that the old caravan he was living in was packed with creature comforts. He'd had the useful ability to charm just about anyone who could do him any good!

Pointedly, she began to pour coffee, both cups black and sugarless because that was the way she liked it and he could do what the heck he wanted with his. Amy suggested, 'Should I put a match to the fire? It's a bit nippy, don't you think?'

She was already bustling towards the wide stone hearth, but Adam's smile stopped her. His smile, Claudia remembered, could stop a runaway train. No problem. 'We're fine, Amy. Truly. Besides, after we've had coffee, Mrs Favel and I will be going to find a quiet pub for lunch, but thank you for the offer.'

This man had acquired authority, Claudia decided acidly as Amy melted away. Lashings of it. But nothing would induce her to have lunch with him. As soon as Amy had closed the door she said, 'I'm sorry to have wasted your time, but I've decided not to do business with your company after all.'

'Cutting your nose off to spite your face?' The slight smile he gave her as he picked up his coffee was a patronising insult. Claudia felt her entire body seizing up, every bone, every muscle going rigid with tension.

Over the past six years she'd really believed she had come to terms with what he had done, with his wickedly cruel betrayal. If anyone had told her that seeing him again would affect her like this—as if he still had the power to give her pain, to make her go weak and boneless with one look from those smoke-grey eyes—then she would have laughed until her ribs cracked.

He drained his cup, his eyes assessing her over the rim. 'I've had a shock, too, Claudia. You were the last person I expected to see this morning.' He put the cup back on its saucer with a tiny click and suggested, 'So why don't we both take a deep breath, put on our business hats, and start again?' He made a small gesture with one lean, strong-boned hand. 'Won't you, perhaps, sit down?'

She ignored the seamless way he was taking over, her brows frowning above her thickly lashed eyes as she picked up her cup and carried it over to one of the deeply recessed window embrasures—because her legs felt distinctly shaky, and for no other reason at all. Sitting down on the padded cushion, she tilted one interrogative brow.

'Who else would you expect to see? Widow Twanky? You can't have forgotten who owns Farthings Hall.'

'Six years ago Guy Sullivan, your father, owned the property. I hadn't given the place a thought until the impending sale was brought to my attention. The name Favel meant nothing to me. Your father...' For the first time he looked unsure of himself, as if he had only just realised that the change of ownership might mean Guy Sullivan was no longer living. 'Your father always treated me fairly,' he said quietly.

Sarcastic swine! He'd been long gone, on that rattletrap old motorbike of his, well before her father had returned that day, so he had no way of knowing what Guy Sullivan would have said and done had he been told—as Helen had threatened—what had been happening in his absence.

He'd got the treatment he deserved from her and from Helen. Had it given him pleasure to hammer home the fact that he hadn't given her a moment's thought in six long years?

But she put him out of his misery in one respect. 'Dad's visiting a friend for the day.' She saw the slight tension drain from his face and knew with a small shock of surprise that he was actually relieved.

'But you are the present owner?' He was leaning back against the table, half sitting, his arms folded across his chest, his eyes narrowed as if he was weighing up everything she said.

'Yes.' She didn't have to tell him any more.

'Sole owner?'

She dipped her head in acknowledgement and he

drawled, as if the prospect didn't much appeal, 'Then you and I do business. At this stage, there's no need for me to view the property; I remember as much as I need to right now.'

Claudia forced herself not to flinch at that callously casual reminder. He might have been able to wipe her from his memory banks with no trouble at all but during his time here he'd surveyed every inch of the property, so no, he wouldn't have forgotten what he'd seen, and decided to have.

They'd roamed every inch of the acreage together, the formal gardens, the paddocks, the headlands and the lovely unspoilt valley that led down to the cove, following the well-trodden path meandering beside the clear, sparkly waters of the stream, hand in hand, blissfully happy. Or so she'd thought.

And he'd obviously known enough about the interior of the house to go straight to Helen's bedroom the moment a suitable opportunity arose. He had never troubled himself to find out where her, Claudia's, room was. He'd made love to her in many places: the soft, moonlit grass of the headlands, the silky sand of the cove, even in the caravan on that claustrophobic bunk bed; but never here in the house.

Had he had too much respect for Helen, been too overawed by her golden, sizzling sexiness, to believe he had any hope of seducing her at all in the great outdoors or the mouldering old caravan? Had he decided his chances would be greater in the comfort of her own suite of rooms, between the luxury of satin sheets?

'So, since the restaurant here is closed at lunchtime

during the off season, I suggest we find a quiet pub and discuss generalities over lunch.'

Claudia blinked herself back to the here and now. He seemed able to operate as if there had never been anything between them in the past, or as if what had happened between them was not worth remembering, she thought resentfully, beginning to burn with a slow, deep anger. Perhaps the only way a person could live with the memory of their own despicable behaviour was to ignore it, as he seemed to be doing with great success.

Claudia rose and returned her cup and saucer to the tray. Her face was calm, icily controlled, hiding the raging inner turmoil. She was about to repeat forcefully her earlier statement that no way would she do business with him but, before she could get the words out, he stated coolly, 'You're married.'

That had to be obvious, of course, from her change of surname and, of course, he looked and sounded utterly detached. Why should he look anything other? His emotions had never been engaged where she was concerned, only his greed.

'So?' Her mouth was trembling. She thinned her lips to make it stop. 'Are you?'

'No. But that's hardly relevant. Your husband isn't a joint owner of the property?' The grey of his eyes was, if anything, even more austere, his mouth twisting in a parody of a smile. 'Don't look so defensive, Mrs Favel. My interest in you and your husband isn't personal. On a professional basis I need to know exactly who I have to deal with.'

He was astute, she had to give him that, Claudia

acknowledged shakily. He could tell she felt threatened—her body language must have given her away. And, truth to tell, she had been threatened ever since she'd walked into the kitchen gardens six years ago and feasted her eyes on the stunning perfection of him.

He had threatened her happiness, her innocence, her unquestioning belief in the intrinsic goodness of human nature. Threatened and destroyed. So she had every right to look defensive.

'I'm the sole owner.' She could see no reason to tell him of Tony's death, to tell him anything other than, 'However, it's entirely academic. Maybe you weren't listening, but I distinctly remember telling you I'd decided not to deal with your company.'

She swung round on the low heels of her court shoes, facing the empty hearth rather than see him watching her with those chilling, empty eyes.

'And I said you'd be cutting off your nose to spite your face,' he reminded her dryly. 'However, if you prefer to take your chances on the open market, and keep your fingers crossed that whoever fancies taking this place on has got the necessary financial backing to deliver the asking price, rather than consider the obvious advantages of dealing privately with a successful outfit like the Hallam Group, then that, of course, is your prerogative.'

He'd followed her. He was standing right behind her. She could smell the cool, lemony scent of his aftershave, the rugged undertone of dominant male. It flummoxed her, made her feel disorientated. She despised him totally yet could understand completely why her younger self had fallen for him, had gladly given all she had of herself, would have unhesitatingly given her life for him had it been required of her...

Claudia swallowed roughly, her movements jerky as she put distance between them. She really hated to admit it, but he was right. A private deal between her and the Hallam Group would save a lot of grief. A company as secure as his wouldn't haggle over a fair price. She needed the best deal she could get to pay off those massive debts.

A quick, private sale would be easier on her father, too. He wouldn't have to suffer the local speculation that would precede a public auction. Having to sell up at all would affect him badly—he could do without the added stress of having to explain why to anyone who felt inclined to ask.

The book she'd been reading recently was lying on a side table. She hadn't been enjoying it. She picked it up because it was something to do, and hopefully it would make him think she was perfectly composed, unaffected by having to share room space with him.

But her fingers were agitated, clumsy, as she tried to slot it into a vacant space on the packed bookshelves. It fell, spine up, to the floor, the snapshot of her and Rosie, taken earlier this year, the one she'd been using as a bookmark, landing on the soft, jewel-coloured Persian carpet.

He had picked the book up before she had time to think, handing it to her but keeping the snapshot. Claudia felt physically sick, her hand going up to cover her mouth. A dull flush mounted his jutting

cheekbones, his eyes glittering hotly as he raised them
to meet hers.

'You have a daughter?' he asked harshly, glancing
down again at the two grinning images and swiftly
back up at her, forcing her to nod the affirmative.

'Look—about lunch. I agree. We can discuss business in neutral surroundings. I might as well hear
what you have to offer.' She would have said anything—anything at all—to change the subject, to take
his mind off that photograph. She swept past him,
plucking it from his fingers with a murmured, 'Thank
you,' as she went. She felt his eyes boring into her
back, right between her rigid shoulder blades, as she
made for the door. 'I'll collect my handbag and let
Amy know I'll be out. I won't keep you waiting more
than a minute or two.'

Back in her bedroom, she pressed her fingertips to
her throbbing temples. If the past six weeks had been
a nightmare, then Adam Weston's appearance put the
tin lid on it! After her meeting with the bank manager
she had foolishly imagined that nothing very much
worse could happen.

How wrong she had been!

Stifling a groan, she surveyed her image in the
dressing-table mirror. She looked haggard, middle-
aged, careworn. She shrugged, turning away, taking
her bag from the top of the chest of drawers where
she'd left it earlier and tucking the photograph safely
inside.

So what did it matter if she looked like death
warmed up? He wasn't interested in her, in the way

she looked. He never had been. All he'd been interested in was her prospects.

Nor did she want him to be interested in her. Of course she didn't. She was no longer a silly teenager who thought the world a beautiful place and the people in it perfect angels. She knew better now. And she could hack it; she could face having lunch with that snake. For the sake of her father and her child, she could endure it and would, she determined grimly, stick out for the best price she could possibly get.

Business, it seemed, wasn't on his mind. And it had fled from hers as soon as they'd realised where they were.

The Unicorn. A mythical beast, which was fitting because it had been here that he had declared his mythical love all those years ago, she thought bitterly as she eyed the tiny, stone-built pub from the side window of Adam's Jaguar.

'Remember it?' he asked now, removing the key from the ignition, and she gave him a blank-eyed stare.

'Should I?' She exited the car.

Of course she remembered it. The tiny pub, tucked away in a narrow, wooded valley, well off the beaten track. She hadn't been back in all this time, but she could have given him an inventory. However, she wouldn't give him the satisfaction of knowing she'd ever thought about the place after that night.

They'd ridden here on his motorbike one glorious evening, scraping enough money up between them to buy a glass of cider each and an enormous, bursting-with-flavour Cornish pasty, which they'd shared.

After they'd eaten, they'd sat outside on one of the picnic benches, slowly drinking the cider, and he'd reached over the table and wiped a bead of moisture from her mouth with his thumb, rubbing softly, slowly, his eyes heavy, his voice low and warm, so warm. 'I love you, Claudia. I want you. Always. So now you know.' His eyes had lingered on her mouth and she had known he wanted to kiss her. 'You've got the rest of the summer to get used to the idea of having me around, loving you, wanting you.'

She hadn't needed the rest of the summer to get used to that. She'd gloried in the idea of him loving her and wanting her. She'd felt exactly the same and had been ecstatic about it.

He'd touched her before, of course, the slide of a hand over her hip, a kiss—nothing heavy—stroking her breasts very, very lightly, as if he wasn't sure of himself, or of her, making her hold her breath with the wonder of the sensations, of what was happening to her body. After his declaration of love she'd known there would be more; known that neither of them would be willing or capable of holding back.

Neither of them had spoken much about that. They'd ridden back to Farthings Hall, her arms clasped tightly around his body, and she'd known what it felt like to be in a trance. The moon had been up by then and after he'd parked the bike he'd drawn her away from the caravan when she would have gone inside to make coffee, as she always did after one of their evening excursions.

She hadn't asked where they were going. She hadn't had to. Somehow she'd known that the moonlit cove would be where she would give herself for the first time to the man she would love for all time.

Only she didn't love him for all time, of course, she reminded herself staunchly as she trod firmly over the cobbled car park ahead of him. Her love had died the moment she'd learned the truth from Helen. And she'd die herself before she allowed him to know that she remembered anything about this place or had anything but the very haziest of memories about that lost summer.

Small though it was, the Unicorn had a reputation for good, unpretentious, home-cooked food. At a table in a quiet window alcove, Adam handed her the menu. Claudia put it down, unopened. 'I'll have a green salad and coffee.' Her mouth compressed. It would be foolish and wasteful to order anything more when she had the feeling her stomach would reject whatever she tried to feed it.

A sable brow quirked with sardonic intent. 'Is that how you've lost so much weight? Living on a lettuce leaf washed down with black coffee?'

So he hadn't totally forgotten. He remembered enough about her to be able to compare the gaunt woman opposite with the eighteen-year-old who'd been blessed with all those lush curves. Hearing him as good as admit it gave her a spurt of savage pleasure. He'd tried to give the impression that he hadn't given the Hall, or her, a second's thought in all these years, and had just now proved himself wrong.

But then, he was an expert liar. He probably had a first-class degree in the twisted art!

'We're here on business,' she reminded him, unfolding the large linen napkin and shaking it out over her knees as their food arrived. 'I suggest we stick to that, rather than descend to the personal.'

'Descend?' He almost smiled. 'In the past, when talk reached a personal level, things tended to go up, not down.' He forked up some of the seafood pie he'd ordered but didn't eat it, she noticed as she ignored his unsubtle innuendo, applying herself to her salad. She managed to swallow some but gave up altogether when he leaned back in his chair and asked, 'Your daughter… What do you call her?'

'Rosie.' She hated having to tell him, but she could hardly refuse. She didn't want to discuss her beloved, infinitely precious child with him at all. Ever.

'Pretty.' His unsmiling eyes bored into hers. 'Rosie Favel. It rings a faint bell. Favel? Should I know your husband?' he persisted.

Claudia sighed. It was none of his business. She would have told him just that, but practicalities had to come before pride. She had the future welfare of her father and her child to consider. She needed to get the best deal she could out of this man and continued rudeness wouldn't do anything to help in that respect.

She stirred her sugarless black coffee slowly, gathering patience. 'Perhaps,' she granted, then took a heartening sip of the hot and excellent brew. He was not to be fobbed off with that, however. His intent, unblinking expression told her that much.

'You probably saw him around at odd times during the summer you worked here.' She refused to elevate the couple of months he was at Farthings Hall higher than that, give it more importance. 'Tony was my father's accountant. He came around fairly regularly.'

'That fair-haired guy who always seemed to be hanging around your stepmother.' His mouth curled derisively and his voice was bitter. Because Helen had shown the young and sexy part-time gardener off the premises, preferring the more experienced attentions of her so-called distant cousin?

Had he seen what she and her father had signally failed to recognise—the ongoing affair between those two? She felt her face go red. The idea was hurtful and somehow very degrading.

'He has to be twenty years your senior.' His eyes were cold, as if he despised everything about her.

Claudia corrected him hotly, 'Twelve, actually. Not that it mattered. He was kind.'

Whatever else Tony had been, or hadn't been, he had always shown her kindness. It was ironic, really, that she hadn't discovered how cruelly he'd treated her until after his death.

'How nice for you.' Adam showed his teeth. As an attempted smile it wouldn't rate one out of ten, and his subsequent, 'So when did you marry your well-healed, ageing Lothario?' made her grind her teeth.

'October. Exactly six years ago. Satisfied?' He hadn't picked up on her earlier use of the past tense and she frowned, wondering, just for a moment, why she didn't come right out with it and tell him Tony was dead. And knew the answer: because she couldn't afford to have him know too much about her situation. 'Maybe now we can change the subject and talk about why we are here at all.'

'Gladly.' He drained his coffee cup. 'How old is Rosie?'

Her blue eyes clouded with anger. Why the heck couldn't he leave it? 'What my daughter's age has to do with the sale of Farthings Hall escapes me.' She bunched up her napkin and dropped it on her largely untouched salad, gathered her handbag and swept to her feet. 'I can only imagine you have no intention whatsoever of making an offer, that you brought me here with the sole objective of causing me as much aggravation as possible because, six years ago, I had the temerity to dump you!'

Claudia stalked out, leaving him to settle the bill, and she was waiting impatiently by the Jaguar when he finally strolled out after what seemed to her to be an inordinate length of time.

'I liked the outraged dignity act.' He was actually smiling for the first time that day. Claudia looked quickly away. That smile of his had always been lethal and nothing had changed in that respect except he used it a lot less often. Round her, at least.

'I hate wasting time, Mr Weston.' She glanced at her wristwatch. They should be back at Farthings Hall in time for her to collect Rosie from the village primary school. She prayed that he wouldn't hang around. There wasn't going to be a deal. This morning had been a painful waste of time.

'So, Mrs Favel, do I.' He opened the passenger door. 'Though I wouldn't agree our time has been wasted—even though more questions have been raised than answered.' He ushered her into the passenger seat and closed the door. While he walked round to the driver's side she wondered what he was talking about and decided she definitely didn't want to know.

One thing she was sure of was the unlikelihood of him making any offer for her home on behalf of his company. That, she reasoned, would have been ruled out of the question the moment he'd realised who she was. He probably still felt bitter about the way he'd been ordered off the property six years ago when he'd been just the hired help.

He wouldn't be inclined to do her any favours. She breathed out raggedly, shifting in her seat as the powerful car tucked neatly into the side of the narrow lane on a particularly tight bend.

'Relax,' he said coolly. 'I'll have our surveyor go over your property. One day next week, perhaps. Our formal offer will depend on his report.'

Claudia did as she was told. She relaxed. Well, as much as she could, given the company she was keeping. He hadn't written off the possibility of a sale, so she could keep the harmful truth from her father for another few days—until she was forced to tell him everything by the imminent arrival of the surveyor. Every day he got a little stronger, so the longer she could keep the dreadful news from him, the better.

A few more minutes and they would be back at the Hall. After Adam dropped her off he'd drive away, she consoled herself, and she would never have to see him again because all further business could be handled through their solicitors. And she could begin again the process of forgetting how very much she had once loved him, and how very much she had hated him for the first few years, and—

'That is Rosie?'

The car had swept up the gravelled driveway and she hadn't noticed. His query brought her out of her bitter ruminations. Her daughter was careering down the flight of stone steps from the open main entrance door, dressed in cotton dungarees, her soft black hair flying around her face, Amy red-faced and puffing in hot pursuit.

Adam braked, the action controlled and smooth, and Claudia practically fell out of the door, reaching out and catching her squealing and giggling offspring and lifting her protectively into her arms.

'Mummeee! Amy said to watch for the car—I saw you come!' That wide, heart-stopping smile lit up the gorgeous little face, the wide, smoke-grey eyes. 'The roof of the school fell down,' she exaggerated wildly. 'The whole school nearly fell down!'

'Just the ceiling in the cloakroom, and only part of it at that,' Amy explained breathlessly. 'But Miss Possinger phoned at lunchtime to say could one of us collect her because all the children were being sent home early. They're getting the plasterers in to fix it this evening.'

Claudia unwound her daughter's arms from their stranglehold around her neck, her poor heart pounding. 'Run along in with Amy, darling. I won't be a moment.' She wouldn't have been that long even if, in her haste to stop her exuberant little girl hurtling off down the drive, she hadn't left her handbag behind in the car. 'Then I'll get changed and maybe we'll take a picnic down to the cove.'

She didn't want her daughter around Adam Weston for one split second longer than necessary and she cursed the fates that had made it necessary at all, and held her breath as, the promise of a picnic as bait, Rosie slid to the ground, took Amy's hand and trotted willingly back to the house.

Everything was OK. Claudia let out a relieved sigh of pent-up breath, then broke out in a cold sweat and felt the ground tilt beneath her feet as Adam said, his voice very cold, very precise, 'That child is mine.'

CHAPTER THREE

'WHAT did you say?' Claudia gasped through lips that suddenly felt stiff and parched.

'You heard.' The dry ice in his voice made it crackle with cold fury. Her stomach clenched in painful reaction and heat scorched through her body and then just as rapidly drained away, leaving every last one of her senses in total deep freeze.

'Her age would be right and her colouring's spot-on. She's a Weston. That child is not Tony Favel's.' His tone was dark, hard, as if what he said was irrefutable—and heaven help anyone who tried to argue the toss.

Claudia's skin prickled in warning. She would have run into the house, locked the doors and turned it into a fortress, but her legs would barely hold her upright, never mind leap into a sprint.

'Well? Not denying it?' His words were harsh and bleak, as raw as the winds which scoured the granite tops of the winter hills. Claudia's eyes were riveted to his in shock. Wide eyes and wild, looking for a way out of a nightmare and not finding one.

Exasperated by her stunned silence, he took her arm, his fingers lean and strong. Claudia shuddered convulsively as her frozen senses came to life. Having him touch her, actually touch her, was far worse than anything else that had happened today.

It was as if he'd pressed a magic button that had transported her to that untroubled past, plunging her deep into her those wild and heady sensations, all that long-forgotten needing, the wanting, and the loving…all those old sensations she had been so sure she had safely buried away like the dead and useless, unwanted things they were, buried away and forgotten, never, ever to be remembered again.

'You're mad!' she muttered through chattering teeth. She shook her head in hectic denial of his basic and frighteningly primitive effect on her, and her butterscotch hair slipped from its confining clasp and tumbled around her face. She tried to tug her arm free, but his fingers gripped all the tighter as he hauled her closer to his rock-solid body.

He ignored her feeble insult, single-minded determination glittering in the slate-grey depths of his eyes. 'I mean to know, Claudia. Even if I have to insist on DNA tests.' His mouth thinned. 'And I will insist, if I have to.'

She knew he would. The cloak of charm he'd worn so easily when she'd first met him had been well and truly discarded. He had no need of it, no need to charm a woman who was near bankrupt. She had nothing material for him to covet. Now all he needed or wanted from her was an answer and he'd stop at nothing to get it.

Claudia shivered in the Indian summer sun. He must have read the defeat in her eyes because he smiled grimly and tugged her just a fraction closer. Close enough to let her feel the way the raw tension coming from him scorched her skin. 'So?' he persisted. 'I want the truth. Is Rosie my daughter?'

Too choked to speak, she nodded, dipping her head so that the thick, slippery strands of her hair fell forward to hide her face. She heard the breath hiss out of his lungs and met the blazing impact of his eyes as his other hand cupped her chin, forcing her head up, his fingers hard against her jawline.

'You knew you were pregnant with my child and yet you married Favel,' he deduced, his voice bleakly judgmental. Claudia felt her heart bang sickeningly against her ribs. Never, in all of her life, had she been looked at with such a wealth of black scorn. And it was undeserved. That made it worse. He, for being the man he was, was to blame for what had happened.

'Yes, I married him!'

It was too much, all of it! To have done anything other than agree to Tony's suggestion that they marry would have been, at that time, unthinkable. 'What choice did I have?' she blazed at him, anger and pain deepening the glittering blue of her eyes. 'What damned choice?'

'You had choices,' he said coldly. 'You found yourself in need of a husband and a father for your child because, presumably, you couldn't cope on your own, or didn't want to have to. So you made your calculations and you chose. The well-heeled accountant would have seemed the better bet. Better than a casual manual worker without the price of a pasty in his pocket! The tiny fact that I was the natural father, had undeniable rights too, didn't come into your calculations.'

He stepped back, dropping his hands, breaking the physical contact that had quite obviously been utterly distasteful.

Sudden tears brimmed in her eyes as she glimpsed what looked like pain flare briefly and vividly in his eyes when he raised his stormy gaze and glanced towards the steps down which, only minutes before, his young daughter had exuberantly erupted.

But then the fleeting insight into the soul of the man had gone, so maybe she'd imagined it, imagined the regrets of a man who had missed out on five years of his child's life, because all she could see now was cruelty, the cruelty that had prompted him to make her revisit the Unicorn, the scene of his declaration of love. Had he set out deliberately to remind her of how gullible she'd been, how utterly foolish, how easy?

She shuddered, feeling ill. How like him to fix the blame on someone else. It was, she supposed, the mark of a true con artist. Charm the folks into thinking black was white then, if the truth ever did hit them between the eyes, tell them it was all their own fault for not seeing straight in the first place.

'Does Favel know the child isn't his?'

Claudia wrapped her arms around her body. Any moment now, Rosie would come bounding down the steps again, wondering what was keeping her, telling her to hurry, reminding her of that promised picnic.

There was no point now in trying to escape the truth. He would find it, no matter how hard she tried to hide it. So she had to get it out before her little daughter made another appearance.

'Tony died in a road accident less than two months

ago.' She made her voice unemotional because it was the only way she could handle this. 'And yes, he knew Rosie wasn't his. He adopted her.' That had been part of the bargain. 'No one else knows, not even my father.' That had been part of the bargain, too. The most important part. 'And I'd like to keep it that way.'

She wondered bleakly if there was any hope of that. In keeping all knowledge of his child from him she had done him a terrible injustice, she freely admitted that. He would look for all possible means to make her suffer.

He didn't answer. He gave her a long, totally unreadable look, swung on his heel and strode back to his car.

'Now tell me all about it.' Amy sat down at the long, scrubbed-top table and stirred her cocoa, eyeing Claudia's goblet of red wine with a tinge of disapproval.

It was her second glass and probably wouldn't be her last of the evening, Claudia thought half hysterically. Usually, this was one of the best times of her long, busy day. Satisfied diners departed, the part-time helpers finished and collected by their respective husbands; time to relax and have a natter, as Amy put it.

Ever since Adam had driven away she'd been avoiding spending any time alone with the housekeeper, dreading her questions, which she knew from long experience would be myriad.

'Whoever would have thought Adam Weston would turn up again like that? It will be too early for him to make a firm offer, we all know that, but just fancy—all those years ago when you and he were going around together he didn't have sixpence to call his own! I can remember how grateful he was to work around the place just to get somewhere to sleep and something to put in his stomach. And now he turns up offering to buy the place!'

Hardly that. He wouldn't lift a finger now to help them out of the deep, dark hole they were in. Claudia swallowed some wine. Nothing for it but to nod her agreement, though she knew she had kissed goodbye to any hopes of Adam recommending that the Hallam Group make an offer for Farthings Hall, now that she had confessed his relationship to her daughter.

He had driven away from her and everything to do with her as if he meant it. There would be no offer, no further contact.

Strangely, stupidly, what hurt most was his lack of interest in his child. Having wrested that confession out of her, he had turned his back on his little daughter, expressing no interest whatsoever in ever seeing her again.

But surely she had done the right thing in telling him the truth? He'd had his suspicions about Rosie's parentage and if she'd continued to deny the truth he would simply have put his head down and gone after it himself, wreaking heaven only knew what havoc.

So this way there would be no waves. He had the truth and he'd walked away from it, and no one would know any differently. Stupid to feel hurt because he'd turned his back on Rosie, indifferent to her well-being, her future, coldly excluding his child from his life.

Stupid, because she didn't want him back in her life, or in Rosie's...

'So you'll be breaking the news to your father now? You can't leave it any longer, not now you've started the ball rolling.' Amy had finished her cocoa and sat back, folding her arms across her roly-poly bosom. 'It's bound to upset him, but try not to let it worry you too much. He's a lot stronger now than he was. It's the business with the debts that will hit him the hardest.'

As if she didn't know that! She was dreading having to tell her father exactly why they were having to sell his family home.

She was going to have to explain to him that not only had his wife been having a torrid affair with his daughter's husband, but that they'd been syphoning off large amounts of income from the hotel and restaurant business, leaving huge unpaid bills behind, bills there was not a hope in hell of paying unless the property was sold. It would hurt and humiliate him and he'd already been hurt enough.

And there was absolutely no hope of carrying on here. A further hefty mortgage was out of the question, so the bank manager had told her.

Claudia took her empty glass to the sink and rinsed it. Much as she was tempted to anaesthetise herself with alcohol, she knew more wine would definitely not be a good idea. 'I'll break the news on Monday.' She collected Amy's mug. 'We'll make the best of the weekend and give him a couple more days of relative peace. Relax in the sun. The forecast's good again.'

The restaurant was closed on Sundays, out of season, and she'd always made a point of making it a real family day, a relaxing, do-as-you-please kind of day. No matter how on edge she was herself, she would make sure that this Sunday was no different. Monday would be soon enough to bring Guy Sullivan's world tottering around his ears.

'Right.' Amy heaved herself to her feet. 'Time for bed. I'll ask Edith on Sunday what she thinks about me going to live with her. When this place has gone, of course. I wouldn't think of going until then.' The housekeeper's face suddenly crumpled and Claudia's battered heart twisted inside her breast.

Amy spent every Sunday with her sister, Edith, in nearby St Mawes. They could tolerate each other in small doses, but that was as far as it went. Edith was too fond of harping on about her sister's unmarried state for Amy's liking, rubbing in the fact that she had a husband and children and her sister didn't. 'It won't need to be for long, mind,' Amy added, her voice wavering. 'Just till I can find another live-in position.'

'Oh, Amy!' Impulsively, Claudia hugged the older woman, offering what comfort she could, wondering how much more misery she could take.

Amy had been housekeeper here for as long as she could remember, always there for her—particularly after her mother had died. And all she, Claudia, could offer in return for those years of devotion was her deep affection.

Hardly a helpful commodity to someone who was staring a homeless, jobless future in the face.

*　　*　　*

'Why does Old Ron like so many pies?' Rosie, dancing at Claudia's side, wanted to know. Rosie hated pies of any description and this Sunday, as on every Sunday, they had delivered two to the flat above the stable block. Steak and kidney, and apple. Rosie would rather have sausages and ice cream.

'Because he knows what's good for him.' Claudia smiled down at the bundle of energy bouncing around her feet. Her colouring—that silky soft, near-black hair, those huge smoky grey eyes—was so like her father's she could hardly credit that those who had known and remembered the young Adam Weston hadn't cottoned on.

If only things had been different and Rosie could have been brought up by both parents, she thought, her throat tightening with unwelcome emotion. But it hadn't been possible.

At the time, Tony Favel's offer of marriage, as a way out of her difficulties, had seemed, if not an easy option, the only viable one.

How could she, on that October afternoon almost six years ago, have known how devious Tony was, how dark his character, what his true intent had been when he'd found her weeping helplessly, huddled up at the foot of the service stairs? In her mind she could still hear his voice as he'd said, 'Claudia? Whatever's wrong?'

If she'd been less distraught she might have wondered what her father's accountant was doing, creeping down the service stairs. Wondered, drawn certain conclusions, and maybe prevented what was bad, very bad, from getting very much worse.

'You—er—you mustn't upset yourself. Your father's well on the road to recovery. Out of Intensive Care and expected home next week.' He had touched her lightly on her shoulder, offering awkward comfort. 'He'll be fine—as long as he takes care.'

Claudia's sobs had intensified at that. She'd known she was embarrassing the poor man, but she couldn't help it. Her father's first and near-fatal heart attack had struck out of the blue a week ago and his cardiologist had expressly warned against upsets or anxieties or stressful situations for some time to come.

So how could she possibly tell him she was pregnant? Naturally, he would ask who the father was. How could she tell him that? Knowing her father's love for her, the determination of his character, he would move heaven and earth to locate the now absent Adam Weston.

How could she tell him that she wouldn't marry Adam Weston if her life depended on it? Pretend she'd had sex with him simply because she'd felt like it, that she hadn't loved him? How could she make herself cheap and tacky in her father's eyes?

And how could she tell him the truth: that she wouldn't tie herself to a man who had deliberately made her fall helplessly in love with him, proposed marriage to her, made passionate love to her—probably getting her pregnant quite deliberately to trap her—simply because her father owned an extremely valuable property? A man, moreover, who had sneaked upstairs while his back was turned and tried to seduce Helen, his wife!

'Look—' Tony cleared his throat. 'You visited him

this morning. Was he worse? Is that why you're so upset? I'll help if I can... Well, I'm sure you know that, Claudia, my dear.'

That was all it took to have her blurting it all out. He was her father's business accountant, practically a family friend, unfailingly courteous, kind, yet a disinterested onlooker, someone who wouldn't be too shocked, or disappointed in her, or upset.

'I'm pregnant! And I don't know how I'm going to break the news to Dad. He mustn't be upset—we all know that! I don't know what to do!'

'It's that odd-job chap's, isn't it?' Tony hazarded after a few moments of intense silence, his voice heavy. 'I couldn't help noticing the time you've spent together this summer.'

She nodded, too choked to speak, hating Adam, hating herself for letting him fool her. And Tony said quietly, 'Let's find somewhere to talk. Perhaps I'll be able to help you decide what's best to be done.'

He took charge and she was happy to let him. Of course, they couldn't talk on the stairs. The kitchens were deserted, the staff off duty until this evening. But Helen, who had earlier retired to her room with a migraine, which was why she hadn't been able to visit the hospital in Plymouth, could appear at any moment.

Secretly, Claudia had been glad to convey her stepmother's excuses, and love, and promises to visit tomorrow. It meant she'd been able to stop off and buy the pregnancy testing kit without the danger of Helen deciding to come into the chemist's with her.

'The chap walked out a couple of weeks or so ago,

didn't he?' Somehow, Tony had got her as far as the arbour in the rose garden without them being seen by any of the staff. 'Do you know how to contact him?'

Claudia sat hunched up on the seat, balling her sodden hankie in her palms. Helen had said it was best to let everyone think Adam Weston, in typical drifter fashion, had simply moved on. Nobody but them knew what had really happened. It was best, her stepmother had insisted. Less humiliating all round.

She shook her head wildly from side to side. 'I never want to see him again.' Then it all came out. How he'd made a fool of her, used her and betrayed her. How he'd then told Helen that he'd only ever been interested in her prospects.

How she'd told him with savage emotion just how much she hated him—but remembering through her distress that it was probably better not to tell Tony how the louse had tried it on with Helen, quite sure that her stepmother would hate it to be generally known. Helen had even warned her, Claudia, not to mention it to her father because she wanted to forget that such a loathsome thing had ever happened to her.

'Claudia—' Tony took her hand and patted it gently, his calm voice cutting through her emotional tirade. 'You're not in any state to think straight at the moment, I understand that, so just listen to what I've got to say and mull it over. Give it a day or two before you decide.'

She lifted red-rimmed eyes to him. If he was going to suggest an abortion then he would have to think again. No way would she terminate the life of her unborn child. Even if its father was a louse!

But her mouth dropped open and stayed that way when he said, in all apparent seriousness, 'I'll marry you. No one need ever know I'm not the father of your child. That would be kept private, between the two of us.' He smiled, his pale blue eyes compassionate. 'I've seen you blossom this summer and, to be truthful, I envied that young layabout. He could ask you on dates, spend time with you. I couldn't. You might have said, "On your bike, Grandpa!" and that would have made me feel terrible!'

She almost smiled. 'You're not that old.' And then the import of what he'd actually said hit her. 'You can't possibly mean that!' she gasped, her breath gone. 'That you'd marry me... Why on earth should you?'

She searched his face with bewildered eyes. She'd known Tony Favel for years but, she realised now, she had never really seen him. He was, she supposed, good-looking in a typically English way, even though his blond hair was beginning to thin and his waistline to thicken.

He had his own accountancy business and an apartment in a classy area of Plymouth; he drove an expensive car and she'd heard the two waitresses talking about him, giggling, saying he was sexy and he could play with their figures any time he wanted! He would be considered by many females to be quite a catch. So why would he want to tie himself down to someone who was expecting someone else's baby?

He smiled, his eyes twinkling. 'Because I want to? Or isn't that reason enough?' He answered her earlier question. He took her hands and held them gently.

'I've known you for years and to my certain knowledge there isn't a mean or spiteful bone in your body. Claudia, I've watched you grow from a gawky schoolgirl to a mightily desirable young woman. And yes, I was jealous of young what's-his-name, I freely admit it.'

Claudia flushed and looked away. Looked down at their linked hands and, almost as if he'd read her mind, he released her and said, his voice reasonable, 'A month ago I had my thirtieth birthday. I've sown all the wild oats I'll ever want to. I want to settle down. I want a family. I can't have children, Claudia—an illness in childhood saw to that. I would accept your child as my own—happily—and I'd be very proud if you would agree to be my wife. All I ask for the moment is that you think about it.'

And so she had, she thought now, watching Rosie dance ahead as Guy Sullivan waved from his seat on the terrace, where he'd settled with the morning papers after breakfast. Marriage to Tony Favel had seemed the wisest solution to a terrible problem.

She'd been as honest as she'd known how, telling him that she both liked and respected him and, perhaps, in time, could grow to love him. But she would never be in love with him. It had been his understanding that had finally tipped the balance, made her accept him, not only as her husband but also as a father-figure for her unborn child.

As for her father, well, he hadn't hidden his surprise at the suddenness of their announcement, as at the fact that she had immediately given up all thoughts of teacher training college. But he'd accepted it. And had given his heart completely on his first sight of his red-faced, squawling granddaughter.

And Guy Sullivan's deep love for his little Rosie was heart-warmingly evident as he allowed the black-haired little imp to clamber onto his lap and demand, with perfect childish logic, 'If you can't play tag any more, Bompa, then you can tell stories. Stories can't make you tired.'

'I'm sure you're right, poppet.' He tilted an en-quiring brow at his daughter as she sat in the chair facing his across the cast-iron table. 'Old Ron OK?'

'As ever.' Claudia leaned back in the warm autumn sun and managed a relaxed smile. Today was going to be as normal and comfortable as she could make it, her own scalding anxieties over the future, her dread of having to break the shattering news of the loss of their home and livelihood not allowed to sur-face, not today. 'Enjoying a good old grumble.'

She didn't say more. She couldn't. The customary half-hour spent with the old man, listening to him grumble about everything from the lack of rainfall to the shortcomings of his replacement, had added to the burdens she was carrying, almost breaking her heart. The new owners would not allow him to stay on in his beloved little home, pay him for 'overseeing' the work in the gardens, allowing him to feel useful.

So she wouldn't let herself think about him, or dwell on the shock of seeing Adam again. Not today.

'Ready for coffee?' He'd been told to cut down on his intake of caffeine and alcohol, to throw away his cigars. He had refused point-blank, his theory being that if he was about to pop his clogs then he'd do it happy, not miserable. Secretly Claudia believed that he refused to follow doctor's orders because since the shock of Helen's death and the blow of her long-term infidelity he saw no reason for living.

'I guess for once I might settle for orange juice,' he told her, making her eyes widen with surprise. And then his gaunt face split in a huge grin. 'You'll never guess who phoned and invited himself to dinner while you were visiting Old Ron!'

He looked happier than she'd seen him look in months and she tipped her head on one side, smiling, 'Father Christmas, by the look of you!'

He grinned. 'Not quite! Nearly as good, though. You'll remember him—there was a time when you were a bit sweet on him as I recall. Adam Weston—a nice lad, I always thought, far too bright to be bumming around picking up odd jobs here and there. I was sorry when he just drifted away the way he did.' He unwound Rosie's strangling arms from around his neck and smiled fondly as the little girl slipped down from his lap and went to play with her ball, oblivious of his daughter's suddenly ashen face, her frozen features.

'He's really come up in the world—he's head of the Hallam Group, would you believe? Nice of him to get in touch, don't you think?'

Claudia just stared, her stomach looping. This couldn't be happening. It couldn't! But it was! 'Did you say—say he was coming to dinner?' she managed, smothering the impulse to scream. 'When?'

'Tonight. You won't be busy with the restaurant. He'll take pot luck. He said so.' He gave her a puzzled look. 'You won't need to go to any trouble. I thought it would do us good—fresh company, and all that. I'm looking forward to finding out how he went from an odd-jobber, scraping a living, to head of a company like Hallam's.'

Claudia could have said, He stepped into dead man's shoes, but didn't. 'I'll fetch the drinks.'

She got out of the chair, her legs shaky, and her father said, his frown back, 'You don't mind, do you?'

'No, of course not,' she made herself reply. But she minded very much, so much so that she only made it to the staff cloakroom in time to part with her breakfast.

She felt like death. Dazed blue eyes met her reflection in the mirror above the washbasin where she'd sluiced her face in cold water. She looked like it, too.

She had to pull herself together. Fast.

She had no idea why Adam had invited himself to dinner. To flaunt his affluence and power in the face of their near-bankruptcy? To tell the man who had once allowed him the use of that very basic old caravan, fed him and paid him pocket money in return for labouring work about the place that he was now in the position to buy him out a thousand times over, but wouldn't because his daughter had borne his child and kept it from him for over five years?

Would he be that cruel? That mean-spirited?

She had no way of knowing. All she did know was that she had to be the first to see him this evening, grab enough time alone with him to threaten to kill him if he even thought of such a thing!

Pinching her cheeks to give them some colour, she stood tall, took a deep breath and went to fix the mid-morning drinks. She then spent the remainder of the day worrying and doing her damnedest not to let it show, so she was a nervous wreck when it was time to change out of her cotton jeans and old shirt, ready for dinner.

What to wear? Her mind in too much turmoil to make any sort of a decision, she pulled out the first thing she put a hand to in her wardrobe. A classic black silk crêpe, cut on the bias to skim the body, sleeveless with a discreet V neckline. Smart, classy.

She couldn't remember when she'd last worn it. Probably for a wedding anniversary dinner. The first? Just a few months after Rosie's birth? Must have been. By their second wedding anniversary Tony had ceased to bother about such things.

As if any of that mattered now, she told herself crossly, fumbling with the back zip. She'd heard her father go downstairs a short while ago, so she'd have to manage the wretched thing on her own. He would put a match to the fire in the morning room, which was where she'd decided they'd eat, he'd said earlier, mindful of their guest's comfort. Although the Indian summer days were unseasonably warm and sunny, the nights could be chilly.

Not that Claudia cared whether Adam Weston froze. All she cared about was getting to him before her father did. According to Guy, Adam would arrive at eight. Which gave her a good three-quarters of an hour.

Thankfully, Rosie had gone straight to sleep, tired

out after their visit to the cove, while Guy had rested that afternoon. She stopped, frozen in her struggle with the zip, her thoughts instinctively flying to her sleeping daughter. What if Adam had decided to fight for custody of his child?

He could, she agonised, make a terrifyingly solid case. Her keeping the child's existence a secret from him, passing the little girl off as another man's. The fact that, after the sale of Farthings Hall and the settlement of the huge outstanding mortgage, the horrendous debts, they would be forced to live in cramped, cheap accommodation while she found full-time work of some kind to keep the three of them, leaving the little girl in the care of a grandfather whose health was frail, to say the least!

The possibility terrified her. It made her heart thunder sickeningly, her mind whirl with agony. And the sound of a car drawing up at the front of the house, directly beneath the window of her small gable bedroom, paralysed her.

But only for a second.

She yanked at the zip and was at the window in almost the same frenzied movement, her worst fears confirmed as she saw Adam exit the Jaguar. Dressed in a light grey suit, casually yet expertly styled, he looked what he was—a lithely, powerfully potent male in his prime with a do-as-I-please arrogance about the set of those wide, rangy shoulders, an arrogance that had never been there when she'd known him, loved him...

Cursing inelegantly under her breath, she took two seconds to stuff her feet into her shoes and another two to scan her reflection and register, appalled, how dreadful she looked.

The dress that had once skimmed her lush curves now hung like a badly cut bin bag on her much thinner frame, making her look gaunt. No time for makeup or to fix her hair.

But it didn't matter. How could it? She didn't care if he thought her a fright. All that mattered was for her to get to Adam before her father did and plead with him, if necessary, to say nothing to upset the older man.

How like the new Adam to arrive early. He'd probably done it deliberately, to throw her off balance. After discovering that she'd kept the existence of their child from him, had given the role of Rosie's father to another man, he would do everything in his power to make life hard for her.

But her headlong flight down the wide staircase paid no dividends. Her father was ahead of her, already welcoming Adam Weston into his home. An Adam who was all smiles.

Claudia slowed down, struggling now for a dignity she feared she had irretrievably lost. She didn't trust this suddenly strangely affable man. How could she?

'My, it's good to see you!' Guy Sullivan looked ten years younger as he warmly shook the younger man's hand, plainly happy to enjoy the company of someone—or so he thought—who had nothing to do with the family tragedy, looking forward to an uncomplicated evening. 'You've toughened up, my boy, and, from what you told me, achieved so much. I look forward to hearing you tell me about it. Rags-to-riches stories are the ones I like best! Claudia, don't hover—come and say hello to an old friend!'

'We've already renewed our acquaintanceship,' Adam said warmly, his smile pure theatre, Claudia thought acidly, steeling herself now to hear him recount the details of their abortive business meeting, wondering hectically how she could limit the damage. Then she stared at him with naked distrust as he covered the few paces that separated them, his smoky eyes holding hers with a frightening intentness.

'Before we say anything else, Claudia and I have something to tell you, don't we, my love?'

Adam slid a possessive arm around her waist, his hand warm against her silk-clad flesh, making it tingle with unwanted awareness. That, and his closeness, the lean length of his body pressed intimately against hers, making her pulses skitter unbearably, plus that preposterously false endearment, took her brain and shook it to mush, making her incapable of speech, of movement.

All reason flew completely out of her head, leaving her brain a quivering mass of scrambled thought waves, when the man who was looking down at her so tenderly stated, 'I know it's early days after the loss of her first husband, but when we met again we realised that what we felt for each other, all those years ago, was still there, and important to us. It just happened. Neither one of us could deny it—we both believe it would be hypocritical to pretend otherwise. So we plan to marry just as soon as it can be arranged and we hope, sir, that you will understand, give us your blessing and be happy for us.'

CHAPTER FOUR

CLAUDIA felt her father's questioning eyes on her and flinched. The silence wrapped her like a shroud. She shivered with tension. What could she possibly do or say? Adam's bombshell had left her shell-shocked. She made herself look up, saw the unspoken query in her father's eyes, the slight frown, and made herself smile.

Apparently reassured, the older man's features relaxed as he said gruffly, 'Well, this calls for champagne!' Then he took charge, ushering them into the morning room where, as promised, he had a fire crackling cheerfully in the stone-hooded hearth.

Claudia's legs would barely hold her; she was actually glad of Adam's supporting arm around her waist.

Her father's eyes were suspiciously moist as he said, 'You're both old enough to know what you want and you've got my blessing, both of you. Of course you have, Adam.' His voice thickened. 'After what Claudia's been through—she'll have told you, naturally, and I'd prefer, and I know you'll understand why, to leave it at that—she deserves all the happiness she can get. I knew you two were sweet on each other when you worked here that summer. I'm only sorry you felt you had to leave so precipitously, Adam. I never did understand why.

'But—' his smile was suddenly wide, transforming his gaunt features '—'nough said. I'll dig that champagne out of the cellar and then we can really celebrate—look to the future and forget the wretched past.'

Despite the moistness in his eyes, Claudia knew her father was happy with the situation. Puzzled by the swiftness of it all, but happy. He had taken the younger Adam Weston at face value six years ago, and liked him, and was doing the same now, taking him at face value and admiring him for what he had apparently achieved. She was the one who would eventually have to tell him he had been mistaken before and was mistaken now.

A sob lodged in her throat, choking her. At long last her father looked as if he had come to terms with what had happened to them both, was beginning to put it behind him and was looking forward to the future. He was a man suddenly and unexpectedly at peace with himself. For now. It wouldn't last.

'How could you do that?' she cried, moments after Guy had left them alone. She had no idea what Adam was up to; her mind didn't function along Machiavellian lines. But, whatever it was, it wasn't good; it couldn't be, because the man who had once been her lover was now her enemy. The scars she had inflicted on him ran deep, apparently.

'Easily.' The smile had gone; the warmth had leached from his eyes, leaving them cold as the winter mists that drifted in from the sea.

He straddled the hearth, his hands deep in the pockets of his trousers, his lightweight jacket pulled away, revealing the sleek black silk of his softly tailored shirt. 'You saw how happy my announcement made him.' He gave a minimal shrug. 'You can always tell him it was all lies, of course. But I wouldn't advise doing that to a man with his medical history—and yes, my dear—' his upper lip curled '—I made enquiries. Three heart attacks in six years, the latest quite recently. I'm afraid I've boxed you into a corner and you can either stay there and go along with whatever I say, or tell him the truth—that I despise you—and get out of it. The choice is yours. But think hard before you decide. You had choices when you discovered you were expecting my child, and you made the wrong one.'

Her head was spinning. All the blood had rushed out of her brain. She sat down suddenly in one of the chintzy armchairs. 'But why? I don't understand what you're saying!' She put her fingertips to her now painfully throbbing temples. 'You can't have any intention of going through with it, so why tell him such a load of lies? Why on earth would you want to force me to marry you if you despise me so much?'

'I don't lie, Claudia.' His voice was harsh, as harsh as the level look from his slaty eyes, before he turned abruptly and pushed a log back in place onto its bed of glowing cinders.

Claudia glared bitterly at his broad back. He hadn't lied six years ago when he'd proposed marriage. But he'd lied when he'd said he loved her. She would never forgive him for that.

'I don't lie,' he reiterated. He turned back to her, his eyes holding hers briefly before slowly and comprehensively sweeping the cosy room that caught all of the morning sunlight but was now rich with the firelight gleaming against the dark oak panelling, glowing on the warm, faded shades of the soft furnishings.

It was as if he was mentally totting up the value of everything in the room, from the Victorian lacquer screen, the delicate Regency whatnot to the satinwood Pembroke table already laid for supper.

'But, for your father's peace of mind, I suggest you do. Lie your heart out, that is. You shouldn't find it difficult, given your track record. He'll be back soon,' he added with a complete lack of any kind of emotion. 'If you place any value on your father's and our daughter's well-being, not to mention your comfortable lifestyle—and yes,' he drawled, his voice cruel, 'I'm bright enough to guess that financial difficulties are forcing you to sell Farthings Hall—you will say nothing, just agree with everything I say.'

And that was the trouble, she agonised as her father, right on cue, came through with champagne on ice and three glasses: there was no time.

No time to puzzle it out, even if her whirling brain were capable of deductive thought. Which, right now, it most certainly wasn't. She couldn't take it in, any of it, much less make sense of what he was doing and plan a counter-move.

The two men were talking, laughing. Claudia didn't take any of it in; she was too busy thinking what a devious, two-faced swine Adam was. The way he could turn on the relaxed charm at will made her shudder. Why hadn't she been able to see through him all those years ago? Too young, too inexperienced, too much in love, the answer came bleakly. Far too much in love.

She frowned, oblivious of everything but her own black thoughts. She barely noticed the foaming glass of champagne her father had placed in her nerveless fingers until he gave her a straight, underbrow look, put an arm around her stiffly held shoulders and murmured understandingly, 'Relax, sweetheart! Does it matter if everyone mutters behind their hands about it being too soon for you to remarry after Tony's death? We three know the truth of it, and that's all that matters.'

So she smiled and drank her champagne as if she were dying of thirst and said in a thin little voice, 'Excuse me while I see to supper. I'm sure you're both hungry.'

There was nothing to see to. She'd poached the salmon steaks and made the salads this afternoon. She needed only to take them from the huge catering-size fridge. But she needed time to herself, some space, an opportunity to sort through her chaotic thoughts and try to find a reason for his monumentally shattering announcement of their forthcoming marriage.

He had already said he had guessed that financial difficulties were behind her sudden need to sell what had once been a highly profitable enterprise. The hotel—more like a country house where the privileged guests were treated like valued friends, where there wasn't a bar or a reception desk in sight—and the restaurant, a beautifully restored and tastefully appointed former barn, joined to the kitchens by a cov-

ered walkway, had, in the old days, been fully booked
for months ahead.

He had only to use his eyes to see that everything
looked a little bit tired now, sorely in need of refur-
bishment; and he only had to ask around to discover
that the restaurant now offered a limited menu only
and was only fully booked on Saturday nights and by
a far less affluent clientele.

So he wasn't wanting to marry her for her prospects
this time around. And he wasn't even pretending to
be in love with her. Far from it. He looked at her as
if he loathed her and had frankly admitted that he
despised her.

She sagged weakly back against the tiled wall, tears
seeping beneath her closed eyelids. The man was doing her head in!

'Sulking, Claudia? Or can't you face not being able
to call all the shots, all of the time?'

Her stomach jolted, nausea burning the back of her
throat. He was standing directly in front of her and
she squeezed her eyelids together more tightly to shut
him out.

'I came to see if you wanted any help. At least,
that's the excuse I made to Guy. He's a contented
man, and swallowed it.' He put his hands on her
shoulders and shook her gently. 'Look at me.'

The touch of his hands on her body sent her senses
haywire, heat raging through her; the pull was as
strong as it had ever been. It frightened and disgusted
her, this betrayal of her own body.

She opened her eyes because she didn't know what
he would do if she kept them shut, releasing the tears

to trickle over her cheeks. She scrubbed them angrily away, knocking his hands from her shoulders in the process, hating her weakness, hating to have him see her like this—haggard with all the worry and unremitting hard work of the last weeks, a dreary-looking, scrawny woman in a too big dress.

He stood back a pace, looking at her, and she lifted her chin and glared right back.

What did if matter if she looked dreadful? With any luck it would put him off the idea of marrying her—no matter what his twisted and devious reasons had been for making that ridiculous announcement in the first place.

'Is there anything about your marriage to Tony Favel I should know about?' he asked coldly. 'From a couple of remarks your father made I get the distinct feeling it wasn't exactly a bed of roses. If you're not still in shock and grieving for him then it doesn't change anything, but it makes what's happening a damn sight easier on my conscience.'

To hell with his conscience! As far as she knew, he didn't have one. 'My marriage to Tony has nothing whatever to do with you, so back off! He was twice the man you'll ever be!'

Which wasn't true. There was nothing to choose between them. They were both as bad as each other! But if he was looking to her to ease his so-called conscience, then he could go on looking until he was old and grey.

'Please move out of my way,' she snapped, pushing past him to wheel one of the trolleys close to the fridge. She was beginning to haul herself together at last. It was as if his mention of easing his conscience had made him ever so slightly vulnerable and had given her some kind of an advantage.

Pulling dishes from the fridge, she loaded them onto the trolley, relieving a little of her inner tension by banging them down with a satisfactory, if childish, series of crashes. 'And while you don't have to put on an act for my father's benefit you can tell me what's behind your lunatic suggestion of marriage.'

'To get my daughter in my life on a permanent basis—what else?' he told her, rocking back on his heels. 'I've thought long and hard on the best way to achieve that,' he admitted coldly. 'My gut instinct was to go for custody, but that wouldn't be the answer. To take her away from you and Guy would harm her, and I wouldn't put any child—let alone my own flesh and blood—through the trauma of being separated from a much loved parent. I've been there, and it's not a pleasant place.' He took a dish of *maître d'hôtel* butter from her shaking fingers and found space for it on the trolley.

'I don't like people who turn their backs on their children.' Grey eyes raked her ashen face. 'I won't be one of them and I won't be a part-time parent with limited and possibly grudging access. I intend to be there for my daughter. So, it follows, if you want to be part of the happy family scene, then you toe the line.

'If you prefer to take your chances and fight me through the courts, then go right ahead; be my guest. But,' he added coldly, 'if you choose that route, be sure you accept the possibility of losing. I can put up a good case and have the wherewithal to hire the best lawyers in the land to put it for me. Consider, too, what such a fight could do to our daughter—not to mention your father.'

Claudia grasped the bar of the trolley in white-knuckled desperation. She needed the support. He meant it, every hateful, chilling word. He wanted his child and he was going to make her suffer for keeping Rosie's existence from him. And there was nothing she could do, not without harming the two people she cared most about.

And how could she risk fighting him through the courts when there was always the chance he would win?

She looked at his face and found no comfort, nor any hope of it. He had stated his position, posted his intentions and knew his own strength. Smiling blankly, his eyes cold, he opened the door and made a slight after-you gesture. She trundled the wretched trolley through, wishing it were a tank so she could run him over and squash him out of existence, secretly shocked and dismayed by her own unsuspected capacity for violence.

But any mother would resort to violence if her child were threatened, she reasoned as he stepped in front of her and held open the door to the morning room. It was only natural. Yet she instinctively knew that Adam Weston didn't threaten Rosie. He had only just discovered that the adorable moppet was his daughter. And he wanted her.

It was she, Claudia, he threatened. And on many more levels than he knew about!

'I thought you'd got lost!' The twinkle in Guy's eyes showed he'd thought no such thing.

Adam smiled disarmingly, spreading his hands, his rangy shoulders lifting slightly, very elegantly. 'Our reunion was very recent; Claudia and I have a lot of catching up to do. You must forgive us.'

'That goes without saying!' Guy was happy, pouring out more champagne, having a ball. 'I can only marvel at Claudia's ability to say nothing about what has to be the best thing that's happened to her in years!'

'Yes, I'm sorry about that. But you see, Guy, in view of recent tragic events, we thought it best to say nothing until keeping quiet about our feelings became impossible. I'm sure you understand.'

'Completely!'

Claudia, unloading the contents of the trolley onto the table, resisted the almost overwhelming impulse to throw the lot at the wall. Adam Weston could say a thing and, by sheer intonation, make it sound like something completely different! He'd probably been born with the knack!

Controlling herself, swallowing a few inner screams, she invited the men to the table, invited them to serve themselves and gave up the pretence of eating the little she'd put on her plate when Adam laid down his fork, hooked an arm over the back of his chair and said, almost diffidently, for him, 'I've got a favour to ask and a proposition to put to you, Guy.'

'Fire away.'

'After the wedding I'd like to move in here, make it my family home, if you've no objections, of course.

At the moment, I'm in a somewhat sterile service flat near the City.'

'Done!' Guy couldn't disguise his relief. 'I'm delighted that Claudia's found happiness at last, but I must admit I'd been wondering how far you'd be taking her away. I'd find life pretty bleak without her and Rosie.'

'Then that's settled. That was the favour; now my proposition. How would you feel if we closed the place down as a hotel and turned the restaurant back into a barn, or maybe an indoor swimming pool? I'd like Claudia to be able to concentrate on being a wife and mother, enjoy life, rather than being at the beck and call of anyone with the price of a meal or a room.'

He couldn't have said anything more calculated to get the older man on his side. If there was one thing more important to Guy Sullivan than the once thriving family business, it was the welfare and happiness of what was left of his family, Claudia thought, seeing her father nod his head in total, unreserved agreement.

'There would need to be alterations, naturally. The kitchens, for instance. Ideal for servicing a busy restaurant and meeting the needs of hotel guests, but hardly homey. I'll be more than happy to foot the bill for any such alterations, plus any other work we find needs doing about the place.'

And so it went on. Proposals and agreements. Her father suggested that Amy be kept on as housekeeper.

Done.

That Old Ron be allowed to keep his home over the stable block.

Done.

Adam suggested, 'Why don't you leave the winding up of the business in my hands? You don't need the hassle and it would free Claudia up to plan for the wedding.'

'Gladly. I've hated seeing her run herself ragged trying to keep things going. Since—well, let's just say things have been difficult recently. And me getting ill didn't help.'

Claudia, drinking more wine than was sensible, decided that her father looked as if heaven had decamped to Farthings Hall and had elected to stay.

He had no idea that all this largesse was based on blackmail and hatred. She couldn't tell him.

Adam was right. He had put her in a corner and the only way out was unthinkable...

'Sweetheart—Adam's making a suggestion and you're miles away!' Her father's gentle chiding had her blinking blearily, squinting a little to focus on her tormentor. He was smiling, but then he did when her father was around. She could do without any more of his loaded 'suggestions', the way he was taking over her whole life and running it for his benefit.

He was probably going to voice the great idea that after the wedding she be taken to the attics and permanently boarded in—for her own good, of course!

But all he said was, 'I think it might be a good idea if you and I—with Rosie, of course—revisit old haunts tomorrow. If the weather holds we could take a picnic to the cove. Missing one day of school wouldn't hurt. Could you square it with her teacher? It would give Rosie and me a chance to get properly acquainted.'

The almost gruff note of pleading he hadn't been able to keep out of his voice was undeniably honest. His need to claim his daughter was probably the only honest thing about the wretched man.

She almost felt sorry for him, for the lost years. Then reminded herself that he'd brought it on himself by his own duplicity, and said dully, 'If the weather holds, then yes, I'll square it with her teacher.' She watched that small amount of tension leave his eyes because he obviously hadn't been certain she'd agree, and felt a sliver of remorse prick her heart, but put it down to slight inebriation.

She would have let her father see him out after being thanked profusely for the meal, but Guy said, 'Lock up when you come back in, sweetheart. I'll load the dishes and take them to the kitchen.'

So she had no other option but to see Adam to the door, not if her father was to continue to believe in heaven on earth.

But Adam was no more inclined to linger in the still night air than she was. All he said was, 'I'll be here at ten in the morning. And I suggest you draft a notice for the local papers stating that the restaurant is closed. If you've any bookings, chase them up and cancel. As for the wedding, I'll arrange that. Civil and quiet. Neither of us will want any fuss.'

She didn't watch him walk away. Closing and bolting the huge main door, she leaned back against it, tears stinging behind her closed eyelids. What had she ever done to deserve the series of catastrophes that had been coming her way with hateful regularity?

'Honey?' The query in her father's voice brought

her eyes open and she tried to smile to hide the glimmer of tears. It didn't work. 'Come here.' His arms enfolded her in love and caring and she wanted to blurt everything out. But she couldn't put her problems onto him. She had to be strong.

'I'm fine, Dad. Really. I drank too much and was too wound up to eat.' And wasn't that the truth? But for a totally different reason from the one he would fondly imagine!

'That's only natural,' her father soothed, patting her back. 'We've both been through the mill—with the accident and—and what we found out about the pair of them.'

And that was only the half of it. She'd hidden the financial nightmare from him. And if she married Adam it could stay hidden for ever. She shuddered.

'Let it go,' Guy murmured. 'Have a good cry—get rid of that stress. It's been worse for you—what with my illness, your having to run this place practically single-handed and me no more use than a dead weight. So let it go, then enjoy planning your wedding. How did you and Adam meet up again? When?' Being the considerate man he was, he was changing the subject, taking her mind off the stress that was in the past, reminding her of what he fervently believed was her happier future.

He couldn't know how wrong he was, and she'd been dreading his questions, had known they would come. And she didn't know how to answer him, so she stuck as nearly to the truth as she could.

'He was in the area and looked me up. We—we had lunch at the Unicorn.' She deliberately avoided saying when. He would never swallow 'the day before yesterday'! 'And everything snowballed.'

And how! She shuddered again and Guy, releasing her, said, 'I couldn't be more pleased for you both—if that's why you truly want.' She didn't answer the query in his voice; she couldn't. With one stroke she could tell him the truth and make them both penniless, homeless, with a custody battle on their hands. She couldn't do that to him.

Taking her silence as assent, he said more briskly, 'While you were organising supper he told me a bit about his position in the Hallam Group. I was very impressed. He's certainly come a long way. Tell you what, why don't I make you a hot chocolate and you can tell me more about him? He couldn't wait to tell me any more,' he chuckled. 'Too keen to help you in the kitchen!'

What she could tell him about Adam Weston and his shock insistence on marriage would make her father's grey hair fall out! She gave him a watery smile. 'Some other time, Dad. I'm out on my feet. And I don't want you getting over-tired, either. It's still early days.'

'Fine.' He gave her a goodnight peck on her cheek. 'Run along, then, and don't worry about me. Happiness is a great healer!'

His parting words didn't help her to sleep. He was happy for her and what he saw as her blissful future. So how could she tell it the way it really was? As hard as she tried, she could see no way out.

'She's adorable.' Adam's eyes barely moved from the tiny figure running ahead of them down the narrow path that wound through the wild, rocky valley, turning and running back to them like a bouncy puppy.

Clad in scarlet shorts and matching T-shirt, her soft black hair flying around her cute little face, Rosie was utterly adorable. Claudia's stomach clenched. She didn't want Adam to get too attached to his little daughter. She had prayed the weather would change, that the Indian summer would give way to the rain and gales that could lash the coast with brutal ferocity, so that this sort of getting-to-know-you scenario would be automatically ruled out of play.

But the day, if anything, was even softer and warmer and she had conceded defeat, phoned Rosie's teacher and made excuses for her absence.

Towards dawn she had come up with what she hoped was a way out of the corner he'd put her in, a way that didn't involve marriage, living with him. Living with Adam would test her sanity to its limits.

'Going to the cove with a picnic is her favourite outing at the moment; it's about the only thing that would make up for her missing school. She loves it. School, I mean. And I don't want you to think you can make a habit of keeping her away,' she said repressively.

She didn't look at him. When he'd appeared this morning wearing washed-out, hip-hugging blue jeans and a soft black T-shirt that clung to his upper body, she had gone into shock. She remembered, exactly and with blush-making explicit details, how it had felt to be in his arms; how she had taken his body into hers and almost died of rapture. So many times. So long ago.

She had craved him then with her body, heart and soul. She craved him still, but only with her body. There was the difference.

So she carefully didn't look at him. Why fuel something she was deeply ashamed of? Something that would become an agonising problem if she went along with his marriage plans. Which was why she was trying to find the right moment to drop her own bombshell and put her counter-proposition.

'I wouldn't dream of it,' he came back dryly. 'Today's the exception. I want to forge bonds, and there isn't much time before I become a permanent fixture in her life. Three short weeks,' he reminded her. 'When we're married I'd like to persuade her to call me Daddy. When she's older and has fully accepted my place in her life, I'll tell her the truth—that I'm her real father, that Favel was a substitute.'

And a poor one, Claudia had to acknowledge. Adam would involve himself with every aspect of his daughter's development; she had only to recall the way he'd involved the little girl in conversation earlier this morning, not talking down to her, explaining about the unexpected holiday and asking if she'd like to show him her favourite beach, listening to her ensuing chatter with smiling, soft-eyed absorption, drinking in every word.

Tony had never taken any interest in his adopted daughter. He'd never been unkind to her; Claudia would have given him short shrift if there had ever been even a hint of it. He'd showered her with expensive gifts at birthdays and Christmas, but he'd kept his distance. Her childish chatter had left him bored and indifferent and her very occasional tantrums had had him flying for cover.

'How were you so sure she was yours?' The words came welling out of her subconscious, completely unbidden. It only went to show how it had been preying on her mind, his seemingly instinctive knowledge, and the depth of her own shock had precluded any conscious prevarication.

She could feel his eyes on her. It set every inch of her skin on fire. She wished she hadn't asked and moved ahead of him on the path, her eyes fixed on Rosie's dancing figure.

But the leather soles of her sandals slithered on the sand-dusted stones and only his quick reflexes, the strong arm that snaked out around her waist, hooking her back against the solid wall of his body, saved her from an undignified tumble.

For endless seconds she stayed exactly where she was, pressed against the hardness of him, the clamouring warmth of him, while rapacious sensations racketed through her veins, every millimetre of her flesh; his hand on her tummy a brand.

'It didn't need the brain of Einstein.' His whispered words, so close to her ear, flayed her. 'I vividly recall that first time. I was unprepared, wanting you yet not expecting it to happen so soon. You were so eager for it, and I was swept away. Off guard. All the other times—there were so many I lost count—I made sure you were protected.'

He put her away from him, steadying her with firm

hands. 'Apart from that, there is the likeness. Not only the colouring but, feature for feature, Rosie's a dead ringer for my mother at that age. I could produce the photograph.'

He walked away, his stride casual, almost arrogant in its easiness as he caught up with his daughter.

Claudia shivered convulsively, rooted to the spot. His body heat had scorched her; his words, cruel and heaping all the blame upon her as usual, had burned themselves into her brain, reviving memories she simply didn't know how to cope with. Now she felt as if a cold wind had blown in from the Arctic, swirling round her with vicious intent. The skin of her arms prickled with goose-bumps.

It was a miracle that she made it down to the cove. But she did. Somehow. Adam and Rosie were sitting on the soft white sand, companionably investigating the picnic hamper he'd carried down. She'd packed it herself this morning, hurriedly, while Amy was hoovering upstairs. The housekeeper's reaction to Guy's news of the forthcoming marriage had been, in her own words, 'gobsmacked'!

Claudia knew she was in for some intensive questioning from that quarter. Amy knew just how recent their 'reunion' had been. Whether to tell her some wild fairy tale or tell her the truth was something Claudia wasn't ready to think about just yet. But if the marriage was called off, as she devoutly hoped would be the case after Adam had heard what she had to say, then that wouldn't arise.

'We're having our yoghurts and juice!' Rosie carolled cheerfully. 'You have some, too. Sit down.'

'Later, bossy-boots!' She forced a smile. At all costs she had to act as if nothing was wrong. Even though Rosie had never been close to her adoptive father and her 'Steppie', her small world had been rocked by their sudden deaths. She had developed the habit of asking if Daddy and Steppie were happy in heaven and Claudia, of course, had said yes, privately thinking they were more likely to be languishing in regions more nether. She didn't want her small daughter to get worried by any antagonistic vibes she might pick up between her mother and this stranger.

So she sat, well away from Adam, spreading her full cotton skirt around her legs, picking an apple out of the hamper and forcing herself to eat it, listening unwillingly to Adam's dark velvet voice as he talked to his daughter.

'I used to come here a long time ago. Thank you for showing me the way again. I'd forgotten how beautiful it is. I like the way the sea creams around the headlands, and how very big the sky is. And blue.'

The cove in a smiling mood, Claudia thought. But sometimes it could be wild, threatening, even in summer when black clouds could pour in and obliterate every trace of blue, gales whistling in, making the waves crash and roar.

It had happened to them once, taking them by surprise. They'd clung together in the driven, soaking rain, defying the storm, so sure of themselves, until, hunger calling, they'd struggled, laughing at the state they were in, back into the valley. Then, breathless, they'd collapsed into the lea of a bank of sheltered wild fuchsias where, seconds later, another type of hunger had taken them, shaking them more severely than the storm.

Claudia blinked the painful memory away, fighting the hurt in her heart, and heard Adam ask his daughter, 'So what do you like best about the cove?'

'Fishing.' Rosie jumped to her feet, a half-eaten chicken sandwich landing in Claudia's lap. 'You can come and help if you like,' she offered magnanimously, wriggling as her mother caught her and changed her miniature trainers for a pair of canvas slip-ons. Knowing that her child's notion of fishing was stamping in all the rock pools in turn, she always brought spare clothes along on this particular jaunt.

'I'd love to help you.' Adam was watching the proceedings, warmth in his eyes. 'You run along. Your mother and I will be with you in just a minute.'

Claudia knew that Adam would remember enough about the cove to know that Rosie could come to no harm. The rock pools she loved to splash in were smooth and shallow, with no sharp edges she could hurt herself on.

Nevertheless, her sense of outrage was strong. He thought he could dictate to her, make her stay here with him. She started to get to her feet to follow Rosie, but his next words outraged her further.

'You've changed.' His smoky eyes, lazy now, swept slowly over her body. Lingered on her breasts, smothered by the baggy cotton blouse she wore. 'Six years ago you were voluptuous. A highly sensual, sexy lady. What happened? Where did that delightful lushness go?'

Her outrage was so great she could barely speak.

He was cruel. Hateful! Her voice emerged thinly, sharpened by pain. 'You might despise me, but there's no need to be so damned personal. The way I look has nothing at all to do with you!'

'I disagree. I prefer you looking the way you do. Our marriage will be in name only; I'd like you to understand that. I'm a normal male with all the usual needs—as I'm sure you can remember. If you were…let's say, as you were…you might have proved too big a temptation, which could have made our relationship awkward. As it is…'

He let his words die away. But she knew exactly what he meant. She was no temptation at all. She couldn't believe how much that hurt. Yet it shouldn't. It should not!

'Do you enjoy being cruel?' Her words emerged on a savage hiss. 'Do you like hurting people?' Sprawled out on the sand, his soft black hair slightly ruffled by the gentle breeze, he didn't appear to have a cruel bone in his body.

'Not as a rule.' He began, unhurriedly, to repack the hamper. 'Perhaps you've conveniently forgotten how adept you've been at doling it out. Can't take your own medicine?'

'I don't know what you think you mean!' The only thing she'd hurt when she'd told him she'd lost interest in him six years ago had been his pride, plus, of course, his hopes for lining his pockets in the future. Unless he was talking about Rosie, which would mean that she was right, had been right all along, and he'd never been emotionally involved with her. Just used her eager body to get what he wanted—an easy lifestyle.

And she proved herself right when he closed the hamper with a snap, his eyes flinty. 'Don't you? You deprived me of the first five years of my child's life. You put another man in my place, allowed him to see her first smile, watch her take her first steps, hear her first words. If you think that doesn't hurt, then you've as much sensitivity as the sand you're sitting on!' He sprang to his feet. Over six feet of male pride, battling anguish. 'So don't bleat to me about hurt feelings, Claudia. Just ask yourself if I should care if I make you suffer now!'

CHAPTER FIVE

HIS words, and the controlled passion with which they'd been delivered, shook her soul. After his calculated, callous treatment of her six years ago, she wouldn't have believed him capable of such deep feelings.

Incapable of speech or movement, Claudia sat in the sand and watched him join his daughter, saw him take the little hand, hold it tightly as he joined her enthusiastic splashing. He looked relaxed, grinning from ear to ear. He looked like the man she had fallen in love with a long time ago. It made her heart ache.

What would it be like to discover you had a five-year-old daughter, right out of the blue?

Putting herself reluctantly into his place—yet somehow compelled to do so—she knew she would hate it, be deeply resentful of all the lost years, all the small landmarks in the child's development that could never be repeated. She would hate the person who had kept her child's existence from her.

Guilt swamped her. She could understand now why he looked at her as if he loathed the very sight of her. The hot tide of remorse swept relentlessly over her body, making her cringe. She didn't want to feel this way, to sympathise with him. She wanted to despise him for the man he was, keep reminding herself of his betrayal because that was the only way she could feel safe from her body's instinctive response to him.

Then, through a haze of sudden, unstoppable tears, she saw Adam lift Rosie in his arms, swinging the happily squealing little girl high in the air before carrying her back to where she still sat.

Almost sick with emotion, Claudia watched him delve into the old duffel bag she'd carried down, extracting a towel and the obligatory change of clothing as if fatherhood were long-standing and not a totally new and shattering development.

'Let's get you dry and comfy.' He seemed totally at ease, removing the sodden garments and gently towelling the squirming little body, helping her into a blue and white checked blouse and cotton dungarees. 'If Mummy agrees, would you both like to come for a drive this afternoon? We could find a McDonald's for tea.'

'Yeah!' Rosie's face was ecstatic as she plopped down in the sand and stuffed her dry feet back into her trainers. 'Can we, Mummy? Say yes!'

Claudia couldn't think of anything she'd like less. But she nodded; she had no option but to agree; refusing to go along with his plans would only make life more difficult for her than it already was.

Yet there was a small spark of hope. After what she had to say to him he would probably get in his powerful car and drive away at the speed of light.

Rosie gave a delighted peal of laughter as Adam rolled up the bottoms of his soaked jeans and grimaced at his sodden canvas shoes. He grinned right back at her and Claudia closed her eyes, shutting them out.

Adam and his new-found daughter were getting along famously and their likenesses—their colouring and that spectacular, heart-tugging grin in particular—were painful. Suddenly she craved to reach out and touch him, tell him she was sorry, beg him to forgive the unforgivable.

The need was so strong it horrified her.

It gave her the impetus to get to her feet, hoist the duffel bag over one shoulder, grab the hamper with her other hand and set off for the track back up through the valley. She didn't need his forgiveness. He had nothing to forgive.

She hadn't known she was pregnant when he'd hunted her down six years ago and told her he was leaving Farthings Hall. She'd only known, at that stage, that her heart was breaking. She hadn't bothered to wait to hear what kind of excuse he would make for his rapid departure. She'd known why he was leaving. Helen had thrown him off the property.

So she'd just shrugged and told him, 'Good. It makes it easier. I've started seeing someone else. Someone with a proper job and money in the bank.'

There hadn't been anyone else, of course, and his obvious lack of financial security, his lack of a settled job, hadn't mattered to her.

But it had been a way of getting her own back, hiding the raw hurt that had frozen her heart, made her voice come out as if rimed with frost, her face stiff, uninterested.

She'd stalked away then before she could disgrace

herself by bursting into tears, pain racking her, remembering how she'd seen him emerge from Helen's bedroom, so angry he hadn't even seen her—angry because, for all his charm and sex appeal, he hadn't been able to get to first base with the sizzling blonde. He had probably never suffered rejection before. Remembering, too, what Helen had said to her.

'Let me take the hamper.' Adam had caught up with her, cutting into her backward-looking thoughts. He was carrying Rosie, the little arms clasped tightly around his neck, her dark head resting in the angle of his shoulder. Practically asleep.

'I can manage. It's not heavy.' Resentment made her voice sharp. How dared he form such an immediate bond with her daughter? She was the one who had carried the child for nine long months, who had crawled bleary-eyed out of bed twice a night to feed her for goodness knew how long, who had walked the floor with her night after night while she was teething, who had cared for her, loved her, put her needs before anything else. And he had just waltzed in and Rosie was his adoring slave!

She huffed and stamped on. Remorse? Forget it! By being the slimeball he was, he had effectively deprived himself of his child. And she'd do well to remember it and stop torturing herself with unnecessary guilt. By the time she'd discovered she was expecting Rosie, he'd been gone for at least two weeks. She'd had no idea how to find him, even if she'd wanted to. Which she hadn't.

With hindsight, of course, she should never have married Tony. But six years ago, frightened by her father's illness, by the possible effect the news of her pregnancy might have on him, it had seemed the sensible thing to do. She'd been too young and inexperienced to handle the problem on her own.

'Do you really want to break a leg?' His voice, hateful with dry amusement, made her grit her teeth as she stumbled over a root of one of the stunted blackthorn bushes that crowded the path near the top of the track.

It gave her the opportunity to catch her breath, give him a withering look. Rosie, she noted with what she recognised as petulance and instinctively deplored, had fallen trustingly asleep, cradled in the arms of the man she hadn't known existed a short time ago, as if, on some deep subconscious level, she knew and accepted the bond of blood between them.

But at least it gave her the opportunity to give him the shock he so richly deserved. So far he had called all the shots; she needed him to know that she had some ammunition of her own, that she could hit him where it would hurt the most. In his pocket. Money had been his motivation before; nothing would have changed.

Then, while he was still reeling, she could put her counter-proposal to him—and hopefully come away with what she wanted.

'We need to talk, Adam.' She was composed now. Her coolness in view of the tangled and contradictory muddle of her recent thoughts surprised her. She watched one sable brow tilt ever so slightly upwards.

'Need we?' Boredom etched lines on either side of his mouth. 'I imagined it had all been said.'

Claudia snatched at her slipping composure. 'Then your imagination is sorely lacking. And, hazy as my recollection is, I don't recall your being this arrogant before.'

His eyes hardened. 'I have never been in this situation before. And don't push your luck. If you have only hazy memories of what happened between us—the seeming intensity of it all—then that suggests a degree of promiscuity that is mind-boggling. Add that to the way you gave me the push when sated, the reason you gave, and I have one more detail to hand the courts should you be foolish enough to risk going down that route.'

He strode past her to the head of the track and she stumbled after him. How could she hope to deal with someone this tricky? A man who could twist every single thing to his own advantage?

'There's a seat beneath the pines.' He was waiting for her at the kissing gate at the head of the track out of the valley. 'If you have something to say, you can say it there.'

She nodded, accepting. He had forgotten nothing about the property. The cedar bench placed beneath the stand of Monterey pines her grandfather had planted had been put there because it gave a panoramic view for guests to sit and admire in peace. He had made comprehensive mental notes of everything about the impressive property when he'd been helping Old Ron keep the grounds in order, no doubt working out how much everything was worth!

He sat, settling Rosie more comfortably on his lap, tenderly brushing a curling strand of midnight-dark hair away from her brow. 'Well?' His voice was low, not wanting to disturb the sleeping child, but he couldn't hide the bite of impatience. He was having to put up with the mother of his child because she was part of the package. But he didn't have to like it.

He was formidable. Before, when she'd loved him, she had never felt intimidated. They'd been equals, totally at ease with each other, almost able to read each other's thoughts. At one, or so she had stupidly believed, in every way possible.

Now those smoky eyes were quelling; the set of his sexy mouth, far from inviting her kisses, was inviting her to beware. She shifted on the bench, wondering if it would be easier to go along with him, let him have everything his own way.

Unconsciously, she shook her head at the weakness of that thought, lowering it, not wanting to see the naked dislike in his eyes. And he reiterated, 'Well? Second thoughts?'

Claudia pulled in a breath, lifted her head and hooked her hair behind her ears. She surely wasn't that weak! Over the years she'd taken a whole load of burdens on her slender shoulders and had prided herself on being able to cope. She wasn't going to let Adam Weston, of all people, turn her into a spineless wimp!

'Not at all.' She glared at him. She could make her eyes just as cold as his. At least, she hoped she could. 'I think you should know, before you make yourself legally responsible for my debts, just how enormous they are.' She named the sum the bank manager had given her; it still had the power to horrify her, make her blood run cold. It would surely give Adam Weston pause for some considerable thought; she knew, only too well, how mercenary he was. 'Add that to the alterations and refurbishments you so rashly promised and you're looking at a king's ransom.'

She watched him closely, waiting for the flinch. It didn't come. Not a flicker of an eyelash to alter his expression.

'So we add mismanagement, reckless extravagance and a complete lack of anything approaching business acumen to your sins.'

Her mouth dropped open, not because of his unjust castigation but because he wasn't already half a mile away, his feet flying, barely touching the ground.

'Well? Is that it? Or do you have anything else to confess before, as you put it, I make myself legally responsible?'

'Yes—' He was going to walk away, carry Rosie back to the house, no doubt to be met by her father who would be wearing that heart-breaking, happy-as-Larry look on his face. 'There's no need for you to take that debt on. What would you gain?' she gabbled, thankfully holding his interest again. 'Rosie, of course, but we don't need to go to the length of getting married! If the Hallam Group bought the property as a going concern, there would be enough left over—just—for me to buy something modest. And if—' She ran her tongue nervously over her lips. She could make concessions, swallow her pride. 'If you were to pay a reasonable amount of maintenance, I needn't get a full-time job. Just a part-time one to keep us going. And you could see Rosie whenever you wanted—I promise I wouldn't make difficulties.'

She could square it with her father. Nothing would have changed; the task of breaking the news about the debts would still be hers, but she'd been getting ready to do that, anyway. She would just need to tell him that she and Adam had had second thoughts about marrying.

But she would have to tell him that Adam was Rosie's real father. How else would she explain his frequent visits, the maintenance payments?

Was she being incredibly selfish in trying to wriggle out of marriage? Couldn't she keep the fatal attraction he had for her in check for the greater good of those she loved best?

She groaned. Adam smiled thinly, as if recognising her mental capitulation. 'Time to go. The marriage stands. Whatever your debts, it's a small price to pay for my daughter's well-being.' He stood up, holding the child as if he would never let her go. 'And remember this. I will expect you, at all times, to behave as if we are a contented couple. Ecstatic is too much to expect. But I demand an appearance of contentment. To all outward appearances, our marriage will work. Not for my sake, or yours. But for my daughter's.' He began to walk away, tossing over his shoulder, 'I want your father to know that Rosie's my child. Will you tell him, or shall I?'

In the event, neither of them had had to, Claudia thought as the Jaguar pulled smoothly away from the gravelled sweep in front of Farthings Hall three weeks later. She twisted round in her seat to catch a last glimpse of Guy and Rosie, waving and blowing kisses in the small cluster of guests who had attended the quiet wedding reception.

At the end of that day, the first full day Adam had spent with his daughter, after he'd finally left, Guy had said quietly, 'Adam's her father, isn't he?'

'He told you, then?' Claudia, clearing the supper things, had swallowed convulsively and her father had shaken his head decisively.

'No. He hasn't said anything; he didn't need to. I think I always knew. What I didn't know was whether Tony knew. Whether he found out and that was the cause of the erosion of your marriage.'

She'd pulled a chair away from the supper table and sat, doing her best to look relaxed. 'Tony knew, before he proposed to me. He wanted a family, he said, but he couldn't father a child. It seemed the best thing to do at the time. I had no idea how to contact Adam—there'd been a misunderstanding...'

She'd let her voice tail away. No way could she let him suspect that her coming marriage to Rosie's real father was nothing like it seemed.

He'd given her a level look. 'I've got enough confidence in the two of you to know you'll make your marriage work. There might be difficulties—it can't be easy for Adam to come to terms with the fact that Tony was around for the first five years of Rosie's life, and he wasn't. But you'll overcome them. I always felt you were made for each other—you were practically inseparable that summer. It was a joy to see.'

Coming at the end of a traumatic day when she'd finally accepted that there was no way she could wriggle out of Adam's plans for their future, Guy's knowledge of his granddaughter's true parentage, his acceptance of it, had come as a huge relief. It was one less thing to worry about. All she had to do now was prevent him finding out that Adam hated her...

Now the Hall slipped out of sight and they were deep in leafy lanes. Claudia turned back in her seat and sighed and Adam said, 'They'll be fine, both of them. Amy will see to that.'

Startled by the first hint of warmth or understanding in his voice, Claudia glanced at her husband of less than three hours. He had changed out of the formal dark grey suit he'd worn for the civil ceremony in Plymouth and now looked too gorgeous for his own good in a stone-coloured cashmere sweater which accentuated the olive tones of his skin, the soft darkness of his hair, and thigh-hugging black jeans which did nothing to disguise those narrow hips and endless legs.

She looked quickly away, hating the way her breath caught in her lungs whenever she looked at him, her voice edgy as she stated, 'I didn't want this. It's a farce,' her voice going thick and husky as she tacked on, 'I've never been separated from Rosie before, not even for a night. And I worry over Dad.'

Staring deliberately ahead, she avoided his sideways glance, biting her lip as he said smoothly, 'There's no need. Guy sailed through his last checkup and provided he takes things easily—and Amy will see that he does—he'll be fine. And as for Rosie—'

his voice softened as it always did when he discussed his daughter '—she and I had a long talk. She fully understands that honeymoons follow weddings. Besides, I promised to bring her a present back. She asked for a Thomas the Tank Engine train set. Isn't she into dolls?'

He sounded fondly amused and Claudia could have hit him. She wanted to be back home, with her family, not here with him, headed for a London honeymoon at the start of a marriage that was no marriage at all and which was already showing signs of being purgatory.

'We know the honeymoon's a farce,' he said, picking up her thoughts as he had often done in the past. 'But it's important that no one else does. It would look odd if we didn't want to snatch a few days alone together.

'So I suggest you stop acting like a petulant child and accept it for what it is—a week away at my London flat. I can spend the time sorting out the mess you made of your finances and you can go shopping. I've opened a current account and a credit account in your name and I've got the cards with me, ready for your signature. I suggest you use them,' he ended dryly.

Claudia felt her face go scarlet. She'd seen the look in his eyes when she'd arrived at the registry office wearing the pink suit she'd worn for her wedding to Tony.

Refusing to spend money she didn't have on a wedding she didn't want, she'd tried to alter it to fit and made a pig's ear of it. So she could understand that fleeting look of distaste, followed immediately by a radiant smile for the benefit of everyone else. He wouldn't want the woman he was supposedly in love with looking as if she'd been dressed by someone from a charity shop with failing eyesight!

Not that he, personally, cared what she looked like. Appearances were all he bothered about. Hadn't he already told her that he was relieved she looked a mess, nothing like the voluptuous young virgin he had so effortlessly seduced? She would be no temptation, none at all. Lust wouldn't complicate their paper marriage.

She hated the way that hurt! It shouldn't; it really shouldn't! But oh, it did.

So she wouldn't think about it. She said quickly, to take her mind off her body's reckless and feckless response to this man, 'Did you remember to give Dad the keys to Willow Cottage?'

'No, I threw them in the Tamar and told him to swim for them!' he answered with dry sarcasm. 'Of course I did! Will you quit worrying? And the larder's fully stocked, the electricity's turned on, and Amy's been ferrying clothes for the lot of them, not to mention Rosie's books and toys, down there for the past two days! Satisfied?'

Feeling a fool, Claudia fiddled with the car radio. Of course she knew that Willow Cottage—fully furnished and conveniently available for rental—was ready for her small family to move into. Hadn't she done most of the packing herself, shopped for the provisions?

Conveniently close to the village primary school,

they would be camping out there whilst alterations were done back at Farthings Hall. She and Adam would be joining the others there after their so-called honeymoon.

Adam had arranged everything. For the three weeks preceding their wedding, he'd booked into the village pub, saying he only needed a telephone, a fax machine and a laptop to keep his finger on the pulse of his business. And when he hadn't been spending time with Rosie—and, because it was unavoidable, her—he had been organising. The wedding, the small reception, the alterations to the kitchen and restaurant and heaven only knew what else.

Deciding he must run on rocket fuel because he showed no sign of strain or tiredness while she looked a complete wreck, she leaned back into the soft, comfortable leather upholstery and pretended to sleep.

And woke when he touched her arm.

They were in a brightly lit underground car park. 'Are we there already?' She felt groggy, disorientated.

He said, 'We'll send out for a meal and then you can turn in. You're obviously exhausted.'

He left her trying to wake up while he took their luggage from the boot. She must have slept for hours, she thought, struggling to drag herself out of her seat. She hoped her mouth hadn't dropped open, that she hadn't snored. Then soundly berated herself for caring and joined him as he led the way to the lift that whisked them up to the penthouse suite at the top of the tower block.

'You have a wonderful view.' She was standing at the huge windows that overlooked the city. It was dusk now, a myriad lights sparkling below them, right up to the horizon, the sky deep indigo running into palest azure.

'I've put your case in your room.' He didn't answer her comment. Her stomach clenched. 'Your room', not ours. That was a huge relief. Or was it?

Frowning, she turned to face the body of the spacious living room. Acres of soft dove-grey carpet, spartan black-lacquered low tables and floating bookshelves, a state-of-the-art sound system, dark leather two-seater sofas.

Very masculine, a little daunting. Like the owner. Who was sitting at the only period piece, an impressive antique desk.

'What would you prefer me to order? French, Italian, Chinese?'

No small talk. No, Would you like to freshen up? Have a drink? Phone Guy and tell him we've arrived safely, talk to Rosie if she's not in bed yet?

But she'd known marriage to this man would be like this. Difficult. Sterile. She longed to answer, Fish and chips and mushy peas, but didn't quite have the nerve. 'Whatever you're having.'

He lifted the receiver and punched numbers. Claudia walked out and found her bedroom. She wasn't going to wait around for him to take notice of her, make conversation.

Her case was at the foot of a low double divan, the burnt umber and cream striped duvet cover matching the curtains. An impersonal room with a small but immaculate *en suite*. Apart from the lack of a mini bar it could have been a hotel room anywhere in the world.

Tears welled in her eyes, and she blinked them furiously away. She was homesick already, missing the people who loved her, marooned here with a husband who despised her and didn't mind showing it. But that didn't mean she had to cry like a baby, did it?

She took a tissue from the box on the bedside table and blew her nose ferociously.

He had called all the shots ever since he'd discovered he had a child. He was running her life, but that didn't mean she had no pride. She dredged some up from where it seemed to have gone into hiding, briskly unpacked, and walked out into the main living room when she heard voices.

The delivery boy was just leaving. Adam transferred the huge pizza Margherita onto a china plate and tipped the green salad into a glass bowl then got busy with a knife.

'I thought you'd prefer something simple. Sit down,' he said, handing her a plate.

The portion he'd given her looked, to her appalled eyes, about the size of a football pitch, but she didn't comment. Why give him the opportunity to tell her it was past time she plumped herself up, got rid of her unattractive scrawniness?

Would he find her desirable again if she regained that lost weight, want her in his bed again? The thought came unbidden and she thrust it roughly aside. Her body might crave the magic of his but her heart did not and her mind shied away from the very idea. Sex without love was not for her and love had died a very long time ago.

Start as you mean to go on, she told herself, and told him, 'I'll phone Dad as soon as I've eaten. Ask if they've settled in. About a month, you said, before we can move back without falling over builders?' She cut into her pizza, winding the strands of melted mozzarella around her fork. She didn't get it as far as her mouth because she had the distinct feeling it would choke her. 'I suppose you'll be selling this flat now you've decided to make your home at Farthings Hall.'

'Stop trying to make small talk,' he said, his patience thin. 'If you're nervous, don't be. I'm not about to jump on you. You're quite safe. I could say I've been there, done that, and didn't much like the consequences.'

'You mean Rosie!' She could hardly get the words out, she was so appalled. He'd given every impression of doting on his child. Surely he couldn't mean—?

'No, of course not.' He sounded, suddenly, tired. 'How could I have the slightest regret about my beautiful daughter? There were other consequences to our affair, Claudia.'

There were silver shards in his eyes and they pierced her. She had no idea what he was talking about, and would rather he didn't tell her because she knew she wouldn't like it. 'You talk as if I gave you a dose of the clap!' she huffed, and went bright pink and wished to goodness she hadn't said that, but then he did seem to bring out the worst in her.

'There's no need to be crude,' he snapped right back, his mouth hardening, inciting her to retaliate.

'I appear to be learning from you!'

'*Touché!*' Something grimly amused lurked at the back of his eyes. 'So let's start again.' He poured red wine into two glasses. 'Small talk it is. Let's see— yes, you may phone Guy, by all means, and yes, I have offered the builders a fat bonus if they'll be finished and out a month from today, and no, I will not be selling this flat. I can run my business largely on the hoof, and from Farthings Hall, of course, but there will be certain occasions when I shall need the privacy of a place of my own.'

And she could guess what occasions those would be, couldn't she just? As she knew from experience he was one hugely sexy man, an enthusiastic lover. Theirs was to be a marriage in name only; he wouldn't remain celibate.

The upsurge of out-and-out jealousy was a searing, white-hot pain. She felt her face pale with the hurt of it and pushed away from the table, dialled the number of Willow Cottage, spoke to her father and tried to sound as if she wasn't crying inside, then went to bed and wept her heart out.

Although she disliked the man he had been and the man he was now, she still wanted him.

She ached with it, body and soul. She had tried to stop it; ever since he'd exploded back into her life she had recognised the danger and she'd tried to stop it. But she couldn't help it.

The thought of him making love with another woman, touching her the way he'd touched her, sharing all those rapturous and painfully remembered intimacies, drawing from another woman the wild and

sensual responses he'd drawn from her, made her
want to curl up and die.

She lay in the darkness and prayed she wouldn't
fall in love with him all over again.

Somehow she could learn to cope with the wanting,
the longing, the endless screaming inner ache. But she
couldn't cope with that.

CHAPTER SIX

CLAUDIA left Adam making his breakfast coffee in the small and highly functional kitchen and went shopping. He could do what he liked with his day; she was going to spend his money!

Which was hardly an angelic thing to think. But she didn't care, she thought mutinously as she paid off the taxi driver in Oxford Street. He had made money available and told her to use it, so she would. He thought she looked a wreck and her mirror this morning had told her he was right.

Howling her head off into the small hours hadn't done a thing for her and the neat grey suit, normally worn around her country hotel when she wasn't wearing her chef's hat in the kitchen—teamed with the sturdy flat shoes she'd brought along for trudging round museums and galleries to kill time here in London—hardly made her look like anyone's idea of sex on legs!

She had pulled a disgusted face at her reflection and made up her mind right there and then. She could either mope around in her room all day, be a martyr, proudly refuse to touch a penny of his wretched money—of which he appeared to have come by oodles—or she could stuff her pride, take him at his word and go out and do her damnedest to enjoy herself.

111

Choosing the latter, she had poked her head into the kitchen, looked anywhere but at him and said, 'Good morning. I'm going out. Expect me when you see me.'

Which could be midnight or beyond. Depending. She might just take herself to a cinema this evening and follow it with a lavish late supper. He had made it quite clear that he had no desire whatsoever for her company, that he really didn't want her around. So she wouldn't be.

She couldn't remember when she'd last been out shopping for herself, and certainly not with a bottom-less purse. And, despite beginning with a belligerent attitude, she soon found she was enjoying herself im-mensely, swooping on things she knew would suit her, flatter her newly slender frame. She floated away from the cosmetics department in Harrods on a cloud of Joy, reflecting that the sales ladies couldn't be more helpful when you pleaded complete ignorance and asked for help. She was dying to experiment with all her new make-up. Normally she was too busy to do more than rub moisturiser into her skin and run a lip-stick round her mouth.

A snack lunch followed by a dedicated hunt for shoes and lingerie brought her to six o'clock and the realisation that the cinema was out. She wouldn't be able to see the screen over her exciting mountain of packages and carriers.

Determined to stay out as long as she possibly could without being arrested for loitering, she found a small Spanish restaurant. She ate her way through a sumptuous dish of asparagus and fried potatoes in a spicy sauce, followed by a wicked number of delicious meringues studded with toasted almonds, a few glasses of Rioja and coffee strong enough to lift her scalp.

She hadn't realised she'd been so hungry, couldn't remember whether she'd had three glasses of wine or four but wasn't going to worry about it, and felt decidedly floaty in the back of the taxi taking her home. Not home, though; home was not where Adam was. But she wouldn't think about that. She was looking forward to a fun girl's evening all by herself, trying on her gorgeous new purchases.

The lift to the penthouse suite made her head spin. But whether it was due to the wine or the achievement of spending his money—as he'd as good as ordered—and actually having a fabulous time once she'd got started, she didn't know.

He was in the sitting room, at one of the low tables, surrounded by papers when she wallowed through the door, clutching at slipping packages, getting tangled with dangling carriers. He gave her a dark, underbrow look and she gave him back a courteous 'Good evening', and clumped through to her bedroom, her sensible shoes slapping the floor.

But her heart was thumping heavily, the awful pain that always came when she saw him shafting through her with a vengeance now. But she was going to ignore it, wasn't she? *Wasn't she?*

She was. A shower helped, the warm water washing the stickiness of her busy day away. She wouldn't even contemplate trying on all those delicious new things while she was all hot and sweaty.

Unstoppering the bottle of one of her new, elegant fragrances, she patted it liberally over her pulse points, pausing as she caught sight of her naked body in one of the wall-to-ceiling mirrors.

She had lost a lot of weight recently but she wasn't as gaunt in the flesh as she appeared to be when wearing clothes that were far too big for her. Her shoulders and arms were a touch fragile-looking, her waist tiny and her tummy concave. But her breasts—though nothing like the lush globes that had driven Adam wild when he'd suckled them all that time ago—were pert and rounded, and her hips still held the remnants of that feminine flare that had, so he had told her, blown him away.

Giggling, she slipped into the seriously seductive new scarlet satin wrap she'd brought into the bathroom with her. She was, she admitted, just the tiniest bit intoxicated from the wine that had gone down so well with that Spanish meal. Otherwise she wouldn't be giving her body points out of ten. She hadn't given much, if any, thought to it since—

'Claudia?'

Adam was calling for her. She sailed out of the bathroom on a cloud of perfumed steam, reaching behind her for the sash of her robe to make herself decent. But she should have made sure of that before. She hadn't realised he was actually in her bedroom.

Her fingers fumbled with the sash. Dropped it. The slithery satin robe gaped and she couldn't move. Frozen by something greater than shock, she saw the dull flare of red stroke along the angular line of his cheekbones, saw his eyes darken, narrow, as they flicked over every curve and hollow of her exposed body.

She couldn't hear herself breathing. She didn't think she was. The air was suddenly thick, heavy, clogging her lungs. But she could feel—feel the tense expectancy of her body's instinctive response to him, the pooling of moist heat in her loins, the hardening of her breasts.

Her resistance to him was as non-existent as it had ever been and if he made a move towards her, even the slightest one imaginable, she would fly to his arms and beg him to take her to that wild and wonderful place they had inhabited so long ago.

But he said brutally, 'Cover yourself.'

So she did, the shock of his harsh words bringing her to her senses, watching him turn away while she fumbled to wrap the satin around her body, tying the sash so tightly she felt as if she was cutting herself in two. His shoulders were high and hard and rigid. His voice, as he walked to the door and finally turned to look at her again, was cold.

'I wanted to ask if you'd like to eat out tonight, or whether you'd prefer me to order in again.' A muscle flickered involuntarily at the side of his tough jaw, his mouth going tight.

'I've already eaten.' How sullen she sounded, she thought miserably. Frustration, she supposed, and her own despicable inability to control her body's desires where this man was concerned.

She had never thought of herself as being a lustful person before. When she and Adam had made love so rapturously six years ago she had been deeply in love with him. She hated to think she could desire a man without loving him. It made her feel cheap.

'Fine,' he clipped. 'Then you won't object if I go out. And, if you're interested, your father phoned around six. Rosie wanted to speak to you but you were out, so I filled the gap.'

So he wanted to make her feel guilty, did he? On top of everything else—like haggard, a spendthrift, a cheat and a liar.

Well, he'd failed. At least the shock of what had just happened had sobered her up completely. She glanced at her watch. A quarter to eight. Saturday tomorrow, no school, so Rosie might still be up.

She sailed into the sitting room and punched in the numbers with machine-gun rapidity and caught Rosie as she was on her way up to bed.

'I've had my bath and my hot milk and said my prayers with Grandpa, before I get into bed. I am being good. I am!' the little girl said when Amy passed her the receiver.

She sounded so pious that Claudia's maternal instincts went on red alert. This wasn't like her normal, bouncy, unsquashable daughter! She could just imagine those big grey eyes going huge and solemn and water-clear as they always did if she was upset or unsure about something. Imagine the droop of the rosebud mouth...

'How do you like the cottage?' she asked brightly, wondering if there was some problem there. Though she had racketed around like a hyperactive flying missile on the two occasions she had taken her with her when stocking the larder and deep freeze, opening every door and drawer, diving into cupboards, excited by the prospect of moving house, if only temporarily.

'It's all right,' Rosie answered after a significant pause and much heavy breathing. 'It would be nicer if you were here. When are you coming home?'

'Soon, darling. I miss you very much too.' She glanced across at Adam who was standing in the centre of the room, his hands stuffed into the pockets of his jeans, intent on what he could hear of the one-sided conversation, her eyes daring him to say one word as she added cheerfully, 'In fact, I miss you so much that I've decided to come home much sooner than I thought I would.'

And just you try to stop me! she fulminated when she finally put the receiver down. Aloud she said, 'Rosie's unhappy. She's missing me. I'm going home tomorrow. By train, if necessary.'

'Rosie's fine,' he said grimly. 'She's not too young to learn she can't have what she wants all the time. She's got Guy and Amy and, besides, what would they think if you travelled back alone tomorrow? That the marriage was falling apart before it had started.'

Claudia put her hands on her hips. She could not believe this! The way he'd been behaving ever since he'd discovered he had a daughter, she would have staked her life on his putting her welfare before any other consideration!

'You'd put appearances before Rosie's happiness? Good grief—she's only a child!' Bright colour stained her cheeks, heightening the intense blue of her eyes. Adam held her disgusted glare with cool grey disdain.

'I would put nothing before our daughter's well-being, as you very well know. You caught her at the wrong moment, on her way to bed, probably over-tired.'

Her glare flickered. There was probably something in that. When she'd spoken to Amy, before she'd handed her over to Rosie, Amy had told her of the schoolfriend's birthday party the little girl had attended that afternoon. There'd been a bouncy castle and lots of wild games and Rosie had come home grossly over-excited, and then got a fit of the grumps.

'And what about Guy's peace of mind?' Adam put in smoothly. 'If we cut our honeymoon short, or if you arrive home alone tomorrow, he's going to worry about the state of our marriage. Do you want that? An outward appearance of contentment was one of the conditions, remember?'

He knew she didn't want to cause her father any anxiety; that was the hold, or one of them, he had over her! She shook her head numbly. She had only agreed to this purgatorial marriage for the sake of her father's and her child's future well-being and happiness.

'Then that's settled.'

The blue glare was back in full force. 'I suppose you think you've cornered the market on "conditions"! I'm not a total doormat, Adam. You make conditions; you lay down the law. You get a child, and a mother for that child, and your freedom.' She was thinking of his freedom to use this flat for a string of extra-marital affairs and her temper was running out of control. Part of her deplored it, but she could do nothing to stop it. 'And what do I get? A husband who openly despises me—a tyrant—a husband who probably wouldn't blink an eye if I fell under a bus!'

'You get your debts paid,' he reminded her coldly. 'You get a decent roof over your head and a life of luxury—which is more than you deserve, given your predilection for overspending. And while we're on the subject of your debts, which, my dear, I have already discharged, there's something I'd like you to clear up for me.'

Predilection for overspending! Was he talking about the amount of shopping she'd done today? Well, he'd told her to, hadn't he? Was he the sort of man who said one thing and meant the opposite?

Of course he was. If the way he'd declared passionate, never-dying love for her, while eyeing up her prospects and trying to get between the sheets with her stepmother was anything to go on!

'I'm going to bed,' she said tightly. Whatever he wanted to 'clear up' could wait. She swung round, her head high, sweeping out, but he caught her arm in steely fingers and jerked her back.

'Sit down, Claudia. I want to talk to you.'

'And I don't want to talk to you!' she snapped back, trying to slap his obdurate fingers away. Which was a mistake because he only tightened his grip and hauled her closer. And that started the hurt up again, deep inside her.

He pulled in his breath; his teeth clamped together. He looked as if he wanted to shake her and was fighting a battle with himself. But when he finally spoke he sounded reasonable.

'Claudia, I know how much you resent me, what

you feel about me, but do you think we might try to act like rational, adult human beings instead of fighting a verbal World War Three? Politeness doesn't cost a thing and it oils the wheels.'

He had no idea how she felt about him! How she only had to see him to feel this wicked, wanton wanting start up inside her. It was sending her crazy with contempt for herself. But he was right about one thing. Politeness cost nothing.

She had matured out of recognition since Rosie's birth, had learned to cope with the bitter grief of Adam's betrayal, with the way her marriage had turned out, with the increasingly heavy burden of responsibility she'd found herself carrying for the hotel and restaurant. She had even managed to handle the trauma of the last two months with dignity and a gritty determination to try her utmost to limit the damage Tony and Helen had done to their lives.

Meeting him again, finding herself actually having to agree to this marriage, had turned her back into a hysterical, petulant child. One way or another, he had always had a catastrophic effect on her. It was time it stopped.

'What do you want to talk about?' She would show him she could be reasonable, too, a rational human being, just like he'd said.

'Let's sit down.'

Rationally, she could make no objection to that. Holding onto her composure as best she could, she allowed him to lead her to the leather sofa in front of the paper-strewn table.

Thankfully, he let go of her arm and she could

breathe more easily. She sat right at the far end, pulling the edges of the short satin robe firmly across her knees. He, she noted, sat much closer to the centre. As he leaned forward to sheaf some of the papers together, the soft fabric of his T-shirt stretched across the taut muscles of his back and she swallowed convulsively as something hard and hot tightened in her throat.

She clenched her hands savagely together in her lap to stop them taking independent life and reaching out to touch, to stroke. Then he straightened up, turned, his body angled towards her, and handed her some of the papers, one by one.

They were old bank statements, she realised sickly, making herself reach out, even though seeing them again was the very last thing she wanted, praying her robe wouldn't gape at the neck, or anywhere else, for that matter.

'Move closer. I won't bite.' The faint thread of amusement in his voice amazed and distracted her. If he was going to be only halfway nice to her, she would be lost. Her stupid heart would grab at any sign of softening in him, grabbing at the mistaken belief that things could once again be as they were.

Rational human being, she muttered to herself, like a mantra, inside her head. And edged, with great circumspection, close enough for them to look at the statements together.

He had ringed the statements in various places. The sizeable mortgages she and Tony had raised for the necessary refurbishments and the addition of a huge

Edwardian-style conservatory. Neither the refurbishments nor the conservatory had ever materialised.

Weeks later, the entire sum had been withdrawn. Adam had ringed that, too. And various other large sums had been withdrawn over the ensuing days, right up to their normal overdraft limit.

Claudia's hand shook. She felt ill, as dreadful as she'd felt when the bank manager had called her into his office.

'What happened to the money? What did you do with it?'

His voice sounded a long way away. She couldn't answer; she felt sick with shame. She shook her head speechlessly, but he persisted.

'I've repaid the bank and settled your debts. Don't you think I have a right to know?

Of course he did. And why did he have to sound so reasonable? If he'd yelled at her, she could have responded in kind, told him to get lost.

She blinked the mist from her eyes, sounding strangled as she told him, 'It's—it's a long story.'

'We've got all night,' he countered, dry as dust.

'You were going out.' She seized on that. He hadn't yet eaten. He'd be hungry.

'I've changed my mind.'

She swallowed the hot constriction in her throat and squeezed her eyes shut to stop herself from crying. He was going to make her go over the whole thing and it made her feel desperate. She felt him move then heard the chink of glass on glass. 'Drink this. It might help.'

Brandy. She recognised the smell of it as he put

the glass in her hand, closing her fingers around it with slight but insistent pressure.

A huge slug. Another for himself. He sat again, angling himself into the corner of the sofa, long legs stretched out, smoky eyes intent. The same look he'd given her when he'd asked her to tell him about herself, everything, all those years ago, while never discussing his own background, where he had come from, what he intended to do with his life. It hadn't seemed to matter, not then. She supposed it didn't matter now—this need he seemed to have to dissect her, force her to bare her soul.

Brandy on top of the wine she'd had earlier would probably make her tipsy all over again. But she took a healthy sip anyway because that didn't seem to matter, either.

It helped, just a little. 'After I married Tony—after Dad's first heart attack, he—Dad, that is—put the property, the business, everything in my name. He thought it was the sensible thing to do.' She winced. It hadn't been sensible at all; in view of what had happened it had been the stupidest idea he'd ever had.

She sipped again, her teeth chattering against the glass.

'And?' Adam prompted. 'That must have been years ago. From what I've found out, going through the paperwork, the business appeared to go from strength to strength.'

'Oh, it did.' A tidal wave of bitterness made it easier and now the words came tumbling out. 'Helen and Tony had seen to that! And I helped, of course, sucker that I was! We all worked our socks off to begin with.

Profits were up; business was booming. I failed to see it was all being done on a shoestring. I was so busy getting through my working day, trying to rub along with Tony, care for Rosie and make sure Dad didn't overtax himself. And then he had another attack and I got even more blinkered to what was going on, if that was possible!'

She blamed herself for what had happened. If only she'd had her wits about her, they would never have got away with it. And she wouldn't be in this position now, beholden to a man who despised her.

'So what was going on?' Adam's arm was resting on the back of the sofa. If she leaned back he would be touching her, she thought frantically, feeling trapped, yet somehow relieved to be getting all of this out of her system, accepting the blame because it had to be hers.

'After our marriage—' she took a deep breath '—Tony decided to give up his accountancy business; it was only a one-man band, but he appeared to be doing well.'

'So I remember you telling me. "Someone with a proper job and money in the bank",' he drawled, and Claudia shot him a sharp-eyed look.

He had never been in love with her and only his prospects, through her, had been hurt, so why should he remember what she'd said in such detail? She didn't ask. It would be safer not to open that particular can of worms.

'He offered to take Dad's place in the business— look after the financial side of things. He had been Dad's accountant for some years. That was another idea I thought was bright at the time. It allowed Dad to sit back and freed me up to look after Rosie and the domestic side of the business and Helen did Tony's secretarial work, among other things.'

She didn't give him the opportunity to enquire what other things. She told him. 'They'd been lovers for years, and quite without scruples. Why should they care if they each married other partners? They could always insist on separate bedrooms and get together at every opportunity, and milk the business for all it was worth. Staff were fired, leaving double the work for those who were left so nothing was done properly. Nothing was replaced—bed-linen, china, that sort of thing. The property needed money spending on it, which was why we applied for that mortgage. He'd even laid the smokescreen of getting several sets of detailed estimates. We got it, the mortgage, and that was when they made their move.

'Everything was withdrawn, leaving masses of unpaid bills, not to mention the outstanding mortgage, which I had no means of repaying. God knows where they put the money—into some overseas account in a fictitious name, probably. They were leaving together when they were killed. We only found out about their long-standing affair when Dad was going through Helen's things after the funeral. And I knew nothing about the financial mess until the bank manager called me in.' She twisted her hands together in anguish. 'They took everything and left us damn near bankrupt and I was too stupid to see what was going on.'

Adam swore harshly under his breath and Claudia flinched. She guessed she deserved that, so she'd just have to take it. He already despised her, thought she was deeply unattractive, capable of ditching a man if a more financially secure one happened her way, so what did it matter if he added gross stupidity to the lengthy list of her other sins? She could take it because she knew she deserved it.

'Not too stupid. Too trusting.'

That did it. A few totally unexpected and undeserved words of comfort and she went to pieces. The glass shook in her hand, scattering droplets of brandy on her lovely new robe. Adam took the glass from her before she dropped it and her freed fingers shot up to cover her eyes. But that didn't stop the tears from falling, positively gushing, and he noticed; of course he did. How could he not?

'You mustn't blame yourself, Clo, you really mustn't.'

So soft was his vocal penetration of her frantic misery and the feeling of criminal failure that had haunted her ever since she'd learned what had happened. The softness and his probably unthinking use of the pet name he'd had for her once upon a time was a different type of torture.

'But I do!' she wailed thinly, scrubbing her eyes with her fingers as if that would stop the tears. 'I let them steal everything Dad ever worked for. I was too bound up in what I was doing to even think to ask to see the books and demand to know why he was letting bills mount up. I never asked why he was systematically getting rid of key personnel—always promising to replace them but never getting round to it. He was cutting corners, saving on wages, refusing to pay bills so that our joint business account would be as stuffed full as he could get it before they stole everything! It was my fault we lost everything!'

She bit her lip to stop herself from wailing. She sounded like a cat with its tail shut in a door. She could just imagine the look of distaste on his face!

What she would never have imagined in a million years was the gentle touch of his hand as he took her hands away from her face, the strength of conviction in his voice as he demanded, 'Look at me, Clo.'

She did, with supreme reluctance. She was still shaking with emotion and any minute now her teeth would start chattering again. And he looked so gorgeous, the smoky eyes intent yet compassionate, a compassion that was echoed in the softening of his sexy mouth. And if he'd thought she'd looked a wreck before, then after that crying jag she would be looking a million times worse. She hated him seeing her like this—a hysterical wreck!

It was unbearable! An enormous sob built up inside her. A prelude to yet another wailing session—she knew it was! And, as if he could see her struggle to contain it, he did the unthinkable and folded his arms around her.

Her heart stopped beating and then raced on, making her whole body shake with internal clamour. Did he know what he was doing? Did he really care? Impossible, surely. He patted her back with the sort of wary restraint she would expect to see in someone who was patting a strange dog for the first time, but at least he wasn't coldly telling her to pull herself together.

'It would appear to me that you had far too many burdens to carry. After all, you were still only in your teens when you had Rosie.'

With her head resting against his chest, she could hear the steady beat of his heart, feel the warmth of his strong body. It did crazy things to her, making her want to wriggle closer, wind her arms around his neck, pull his head down to kiss her.

But he would hate that, she reminded herself sadly, and to take her mind off what she wanted she said, a touch tartly, 'I grew up fast.'

'I guess you had to.' Was that grudging admiration in his voice? Oh, surely not. She was off her head even to imagine such a thing.

She had to remember, at all times—even at times like this when he had put his loathing of her momentarily to one side in order to offer comfort—that he neither respected nor admired her and that all he wanted of her was a paper wife who knew her place and stayed in it. And his daughter, of course.

'Clo, listen to me. You were overburdened; your husband took over the financial aspect of the business, which, apparently, he was well qualified to do. Why would you have tried to muscle in on his job when you had more than enough of your own work to do? Why shouldn't you have trusted him? Being a devious louse, he would have been pretty smart when it came to covering up, so there's no earthly reason why you should blame yourself. And you have nothing to worry about now.' He had been holding her, but stiffly. Now the tension left his body and he gathered her closer. 'Your home is safe and your father need never know how close he came to losing it.'

Claudia's head was swimming, her breathing shallow. Her breasts were beginning to peak and strain against his chest in silent invitation. What this man did to her was nothing short of actionable! And there seemed to be no way on earth she could fight it.

She slid her hands up over his body, resting them on his shoulders, and her voice was husky.

'I know. Adam—I appreciate what you've done. I guess I haven't seemed very grateful—but I am.' She inched her hands down, her fingers splayed, until they came to rest just above the place where her breasts were pressed against his body. She ached for him to touch them, to take the aroused tips into the hot moisture of his mouth and suckle her. The remembered sensations were sending her wild.

She wriggled her hips, moving closer, and his heart was beating faster now; she could feel it beneath her fingers. Was he remembering too? Remembering the way it had been for them, the sheer magical, ecstatic mystery of it all?

'You don't have to be grateful. I gained as well, remember?' His voice sounded thick, as if he too was breathing too shallowly, too fast. He lowered his head until it was a hair's breadth away from hers as his hands began to slide over her, from the nape of her neck to the flare of her hips and slowly back again, stroking her through the slinky, slithery satin. 'I've been too hard on you in that respect. I didn't know why the business had got in such a mess.' With every word he said his voice was growing more slurred, and it wasn't because of the brandy—he'd barely touched it. 'They gave you a hell of a rough ride between them—that louse of a husband and that bitch Helen.'

Hearing that woman's name on his lips should have brought her to her senses. But it didn't. Nothing could now. Her need for him was as uninhibited, as eager and hedonistic as it had been when she'd first catapulted into love.

She only had to move her head a fraction and their lips would be touching, and then everything would be as it had been before: the hunger of his mouth on hers; the sheer ecstasy of every exploratory caress; the desire that was never sated no matter how many times their eager bodies were joined in the wild music of love; the fact that it just got better every time. The temptation was too great, too much to handle. Her lips parted…

He put her away from him with hands that were suddenly hard and impersonal. He stood up awkwardly and went to the drinks tray, pouring himself another brandy, which he downed in one long swallow.

Claudia didn't know where she was. Everything had got turned on its head. She watched his back with huge, unblinking eyes, feeling the heat of desire drain away, leaving her cold.

She shivered. She had been so sure he had felt it, too. All the old magic. She had believed for a few moments that it had all come back. But how could it come back when it had never been there in the first place? Not for him.

She had made such a fool of herself and she was

still shivering when he eventually turned back to her, fresh brandy in his glass. And of course he hadn't been moved, or only by a slight feeling of remorse, because his voice was back to normal, even slightly more clipped than it usually was.

'I think you were right. If Rosie's missing you then we should go back. Tomorrow. I'll come up with something to make our early return seem reasonable. I'll dive out first thing while you pack and pick up a gift to take back for her, so if I'm not around when you get up you'll know where I am.' He lowered his eyes under the intense blue of her stare. For the first time in her life she saw him at what appeared to be a disadvantage.

Embarrassed? Embarrassed by the quivering expectancy he'd felt as he'd touched her? He'd only meant to be kind, to reassure her, and she'd practically sizzled with banked-down desires all ready to explode in his face. So he'd backed off. She could hardly blame him.

She felt ridiculous. She had humiliated herself. He said calmly, 'Why don't you go to bed? We've a long drive in the morning.'

She stood up, clutching at her robe, wishing she were wearing anything but this seductive thing. Should she apologise for clinging to him the way she had, put it down to being over-emotional because of what he'd made her tell him? She licked her lips and he said, harshly now, 'For goodness' sake, Claudia. Go to bed.'

CHAPTER SEVEN

'MUMMY! Daddy!' Rosie came flying down the path to greet them, arriving at the garden gate before Adam had turned off the ignition.

Claudia's heart jerked. Oh, how she had missed this small scrap of exuberance—and how naturally she had taken to calling Adam 'Daddy'! She had only been invited to, and only if she wanted to, at the small reception after their low-key wedding.

She was wearing a chunky pink sweater and a diminutive pair of red cords. She'd been playing in the garden, and the now chilly autumn air had brought a rosy glow to her cheeks, an extra sparkle to her huge grey eyes. She was doing her best to climb over the garden gate and Claudia scrambled out of the car and over the pavement to open the gate and scoop her tiny daughter up in her arms.

'Is anything wrong?' Guy, looking bewildered, asked from the doorstep, drawn out, no doubt, to investigate Rosie's delighted shrieks. 'I thought you were staying away for a week.'

'Nothing's wrong.' Adam joined Claudia on the path, smiling into his daughter's merry eyes. 'Hello, scrap.' He indicated the package he held under one arm and put the other round Claudia's shoulders. 'We've got something for you; we remembered our promise!' Then, smiling at Guy, he said, 'Unfortunately, something cropped up. Something my PA believes only I can handle. But I'll make it up to you, Clo; you know I will.'

The warmly intimate look he turned on her took her breath away. But that, and the slow, heart-stopping smile, was for her father's benefit. As was the lie that came tripping so easily off his tongue. For his peace of mind Guy had to continue to believe that this was a marriage made in heaven, that his beloved only child had found real happiness at last.

Rosie slithered out of her arms, intent on getting her hands on the promised gift, and Adam said, grinning, 'Back in the house, scrap. You can open your present inside,' and followed the scampering feet, leaving Claudia to trudge behind.

The journey from London had been largely silent except when they'd stopped at one of the motorway service areas for lunch. Then they'd made small talk, but she'd still felt embarrassed over her behaviour of the evening before and he'd seemed lost in his own thoughts.

She still had no clear idea why he'd abruptly changed his mind about returning today. Perhaps he'd repented of his out-of-hand dismissal of her statement that Rosie was missing her mum.

In view of his kindness, the way he'd reassured her that the financial mess she'd been in had been none of her making, she could almost believe so. His heart was in the right place, sometimes. Certainly where his daughter was concerned. A smile curved her soft lips as she watched Rosie tug at her new daddy's hand, urging him over the doorstep to Willow Cottage.

Guy, walking at her side, said, 'Amy's down at the village shop, but I can rustle something up if you're hungry.'

'We stopped on the way, Dad.' She tucked her hand through his arm as they walked into the tiny hall together. There was no sign of Adam or Rosie but she could hear them through the closed sitting-room door, the little girl's excited babblings and Adam's deeper voice, warm with affection. 'But a cup of tea would be nice. I'll make it, though. How have you been?'

'Absolutely fine,' he assured her, giving the hand that rested on his arm a comforting pat. 'I haven't felt this relaxed in years. It's a relief not to have to consider the business. And I never thought I'd hear myself saying this, but after all those years of having other people—strangers most of 'em—in our home and paying for the privilege it will be nice to have it just to ourselves, enjoy Farthings Hall as a proper home. Which, of course, is all down to that husband of yours.'

Her heart plummeted. Did he know that they had almost lost everything? How could he know? If he did know, then he had weathered the shock far better than she could have expected.

But, 'He made sure the builders don't hang about! I drove up this morning and they're certainly shifting. I suppose they're glad of the overtime. Said they'd be working tomorrow, too. It would have felt a bit funny living there with the kitchens as they were, and a restaurant full of empty tables!'

So that was what he'd meant. Claudia gave a tiny sigh of relief. She would hate for her father ever to have to face the full truth of Helen's cruelty, face the final truth of his dead wife's complete lack of caring or concern, the way she'd been happy to leave him bankrupt, thrown out of his home with no place to go but down.

'It's a pity about having to cut short your honeymoon,' Guy said, apparently content to stay out in the hallway, chatting for hours. But, Claudia realised, he probably wanted her assurance that everything was fine, that the so-called honeymoon hadn't turned out to be such a disaster that they'd given up on it so quickly.

She gave it, forcing herself to smile. 'Yes, well, I guess that being married to the chief executive of a booming company does have its occasional downside! We'll probably take off next spring to make up for it—in the Easter holidays, maybe, so we can take Rosie along as well. And Adam and I have the rest of our lives together, don't forget—so it hardly matters if our honeymoon only lasted a couple of days!'

She sounded perky, but her heart ached. The rest of their lives together. Yet miles and miles apart when it came right down to it. She didn't know how she could endure it if this delinquent need for him, this turbulent wanting, didn't lie down, curl up and die. She had to keep reminding herself of what had happened in the past, how he had betrayed her, used her, telling herself she'd done the right thing in cutting him out of her life. If she didn't do that she would humiliate herself by falling in love with him all over again.

Thankfully, Guy appeared to be totally reassured.

He was beaming happily as he said, 'Will you just listen to that child?'

The excited chatter had given way to loud choo-choo noises. 'I'll make that tea,' Claudia said.

When she carried the tray through to the cosy sitting-room, the three of them were on the floor playing with the train set. Adam levered himself up reluctantly, accepting a cup. 'I'll have to go when I've had this. I'll miss you, Clo, but I'll be back just as soon as I can.'

She knew he didn't mean it, the missing her bit, nevertheless it did something to her heart and filled it with an emotion she wasn't up to examining too closely. But she had to go with him to his car; it would have looked odd if she hadn't.

Rosie wanted to go, too, but Guy held her back. 'It's raining, poppet. Stay with Gramps and play with your train set; show me how it works.'

It was, too. A fine, cold drizzle. The glorious Indian summer had gone and winter was round the corner. Winter in her heart, too, as he stood at the nearside of his car, jiggling his keys, silver ice in his eyes, frost in his voice.

'I don't know how long I'll be away. I'll phone you. I'll put some feelers out and see what I can do to trace that embezzled money. Go back inside before you get soaked.'

That was why he'd cut their smokescreen honeymoon short. Money. Not as a concession to her or Rosie's feelings.

Just money. He'd been prepared to shell out an enormous sum in order to get his daughter into his life on a permanent basis. But the prospect of getting it back had him forgetting his daughter and the need to keep up a front of a supposedly happy marriage and haring off into the distance like a pig after truffles.

Over the following days that thought kept coming back to her whenever she had an unoccupied moment. Amy said, 'You're pining for him, aren't you?' and Claudia didn't disabuse her. The woman who had been like a mother to her in many ways knew her too well. Claudia guessed the older woman was fully aware—as her father had been—that Adam was Rosie's real father.

Thankfully, she'd held her tongue on that particular subject. Claudia didn't think she could talk about it without breaking down and revealing her present misery. But she knew it couldn't be too long before Amy's curiosity got the better of her.

'Yes,' she said, gathering up her wits. 'But he said he wouldn't be away for much longer.'

He'd been gone nearly two weeks and every early evening when he made his duty phone call he said, 'Just tell them the problem's more involved than I thought,' and asked to speak to Rosie.

She had left her father reading in the sitting room in front of the fire and had come to the kitchen to get on with the ironing. She'd finished now, and folded up the board, and Amy, popping the pie she'd made for supper into the fridge, offered, 'How about a nice cup of tea? Your dad will be ready for one, if I know him!'

Claudia shook her head as the sudden need to get away from here swamped her. Every day of his absence brought increasing restlessness, an inner agitation that got worse with each passing hour.

'I thought I'd drive up to the Hall and check on the builders' progress.' She needed time alone. She'd check up on the work, of course, so that she could report back, but then she'd give the men a wide berth, find a quiet place and try to talk herself into some kind of acceptance of the way things were and were always going to be, an acceptance of Adam's bleak indifference.

'Would you pick Rosie up from school?' No hardship there, the village primary was so near. 'And give her her tea? I don't know exactly how long I'll be.'

'Of course I will. It's exciting, isn't it? It's going to be really lovely when we move back in. And don't you fret about that husband of yours—he won't spend a moment more than he has to away from you and Rosie!'

Claudia grabbed her padded coat from the utility room and fled.

It wasn't far, just a few miles, and after parking on the gravelled sweep she went to check on Old Ron. He insisted she take a cup of tea with him. She tried not to shudder as the powerful brew went down and couldn't help smiling when he assured her he was keeping an eye on them blighters, just to see they put they's back behind the job and didn't skip no corners!

What the workmen would think of that dour presence, hovering and watching every move they made, didn't bear thinking about. They had her sympathy!

The lightening of her mood was brief. She didn't bother inspecting progress in the former restaurant.

Redesigning the interior, excavating the pool, sorting out the heating and draining systems would take quite a while but the kitchen had been transformed.

The rows of professional hotplates, ovens and burners, the stainless-steel work surfaces and wooden chopping blocks had disappeared. Unglazed terracotta tiles rang sweetly beneath her feet; the shiny bright red Aga Amy had insisted on was already installed and there was a wealth of cupboards and fixed dressers sympathetically created from reclaimed pine.

The atmospheric country kitchen Amy had always dreamed of was coming to life. But what of her own dreams?

Claudia turned away from the workmen who had paused only long enough to give her a progress report; turned away quickly before any of them could see the sudden glitter of tears in her eyes.

She had no dreams. She couldn't afford to let herself have dreams.

The man she had loved had never existed. The man she had loved had been perfection. A fantasy, someone he'd created for her. The reality had been vastly different, as she'd learned from Helen.

Pausing on her way up the wide oak staircase, she felt her heart turn over in her chest. Could she really trust Helen's word?

Her stepmother had been a cheat, a thief who had plotted with her lover to take everything away from her cuckolded husband, leaving him with next to nothing. Had she told the truth, all those years ago, about what Adam had done and said?

For a moment she was filled with the brightness of

glorious hope and then it went, like a heavy door slamming in her face.

She walked on slowly, a white-knuckled hand gripping the carved bannister, her legs leaden. Even if she decided to discount completely what Helen had said, she'd had the evidence of her own eyes. She'd seen Adam walking out of her stepmother's room, slamming the door behind him, his face black with anger, his eyes too blind with rage even to see her.

She'd started to go after him as he'd stridden towards the main staircase, but had thought better of it. She'd never seen him angry before; didn't think she'd ever seen anyone quite that angry. So she'd gone straight into Helen's room and been appalled by what she'd heard.

Helen had had no reason to lie, not in that instance. She would have had nothing to gain. And of course Adam had been in a blind temper. He'd been sexually rejected and thrown out of his job in one breath! Only after her stepmother's death, such a relatively short time ago, had she learned what the woman was capable of—the lies, the deceit. It would be too easy now, with hindsight, to make herself believe she'd lied about what Adam had said and done. But she couldn't blind herself to the fact that Helen would have had nothing to gain by inventing such a story.

She reached the room that had been hers since childhood and switched on the light. For a moment she leaned back against the door, willing the emptiness to go away. An emptiness that seemed far greater after she'd allowed herself that moment of hope.

Then she crossed to the window-seat and watched the afternoon light fade from the sky.

It was completely dark when she heard the workmen leave. She'd told them she'd lock up so that wasn't a problem; she wouldn't find herself a prisoner, locked in, until they came back in the morning.

Even so, it was time she made a move. She rose, blinking, stretching the stiffness from her body. Far from finding an acceptance of her unenviable position as Adam's paper wife over the past hour or so, her mind had remained stubbornly blank.

She supposed her overwrought emotions had needed the respite. She had the rest of her life to come to terms with her situation, accept that Adam would never forgive her for keeping his child's existence from him, that he would always regard her, the mother of his child, as a necessary evil. She knew it shouldn't matter, that his betrayal of six years ago should make his opinion of her immaterial. But it did matter because it hurt like hell.

She walked to the door, but it opened before she got there.

He looked drawn, as if he hadn't slept for a week, as if he had something on his mind that had been draining the life force from him.

Raindrops spangled his silky dark hair, glistened on the shoulders of his soft leather jacket. Claudia's heart gave a sickening lurch then fluttered on in panic, making her breath catch in her throat. She ached to cradle his head against her breast, kiss the lines of weariness from his face. No matter what he'd done to her, the misery he'd created, she still loved him. That was the stark truth she'd been hiding from. And now she was going to have to cope with it.

'They told me you were here. That I might catch you before you started back.' He closed the door behind him, silver eyes intent on her frozen face. His mouth tightened. 'Nothing to say? Not even, How are you and did you have a good trip?'

She opened her mouth, but no words came. Yet her mind was shrieking. She was no longer a silly eighteen-year-old, putty in the hands of a handsome charmer, enthusiastically falling in love with a man who had a cash register where his heart should have been. She couldn't still be in love with him. She couldn't!

'I—I didn't expect you,' she managed to blurt out. 'Did you call in at the cottage?'

Stupid question! She deserved his dry, 'Naturally. How else would I have known where to find you? I arrived in time to have tea with Rosie and hear her read and let her beat me at Ludo twice.' A smile flickered briefly as if, finding himself in an unpleasant situation, he was recalling one he had enjoyed. 'I said I'd collect you and take you out for supper. Amy was of the opinion that you'd want to go back and change, but I told her you wouldn't bother; it wasn't important. We'd find a quiet pub somewhere for a snack.' He eyed her narrowly. 'They'd expect us to want to spend time together, on our own. It seemed to be the right impression to give.'

He was good at giving impressions. Claudia turned away, not wanting him to see the hurt on her face.

How easily he could make other people see him the way he wanted them to. Only she knew the real man behind the charming, considerate façade.

'I'm not hungry,' she stated woodenly.

'No. Neither am I.' He sighed. He had moved, was standing close behind her. The electrical storm that always shook her when he was near made her legs turn to water. She took herself back to the window seat and sank down gratefully, her breath coming in shallow, ragged gasps as she watched him take in the details of the tiny room that had always been hers, the soft colours of the pale blue and lemon sprigged wallpaper, the virginal white cover on the narrow bed, and willed him to go away and leave her in peace—or as much peace as she could ever hope to attain.

But he said, 'There's something I want to ask you.' He sat on the edge of the bed, facing her now, his eyes bleak. 'I'll understand if you refuse to answer because under the circumstances I probably have no right to know.' He inhaled harshly. 'Tell me about Tony.'

Her eyes went wide. It was the last thing she had expected. 'What about him? You already know he was a liar and a thief. What else is there you need to know?'

He gave her a level look. 'Your relationship. How was it? Was he good in bed? Did he satisfy you? Although I have only the vaguest of recollections of the man, I wouldn't think so. He was sneaking off to be with Helen at every opportunity and you, as I vividly recall, were exuberantly sexy…'

He let the implication hang on the air and Claudia

shot to her feet. She didn't have to stay and listen to this! She would have liked to slap his face but wouldn't demean herself. She would just walk out!

'Do you get your kicks out of being cruel?' she snapped through her teeth as she marched past him, but his hand snaked out, looping around her hips, pulling her down beside him on the bed. 'I don't have to tell you a thing!' she managed, just as soon as she got her breath back. 'You said so!'

'I think you just did. Answer it, I mean.'

He wasn't letting her go. If anything, his arm had tightened around her tense body. She was holding herself stiffly, too afraid to relax. This close to him, she didn't trust herself. Despite everything, her instinct was to turn to him, burrow into the warm, exciting maleness of him, forget everything but the sheer magic of him.

Madness. Dangerous madness!

The threat to her sanity grew worse when he said gruffly, 'I had to know. I needed to know. If you think I was being cruel, then you don't know the half of it. I always thought that the physical side of our relationship was very special, something that only happens once in a lifetime—and then only if you happen to get lucky. I hated to think of Favel—'

'Don't tell me you're jealous!' she injected scornfully, unable to bear the sudden rush of memories. Knowing that he remembered, too, made it so painfully poignant. But his memories would be different from hers. Hers were of long, perfumed summer nights filled with love. His would be memories of the same nights filled with great sex. All spiced up with his hopes of becoming the husband of the heir to a valuable property.

'Claudia—as I've said before, we don't have to turn every private encounter into a battle.' He released her. He sounded incredibly weary. She didn't move, even though she could have done now, sudden lethargy taking over. And he was right. Life would be even more untenable if every time they met they went for the jugular.

She had nothing to lose by telling him the truth. In a way it would be a relief to unburden herself. Then, perhaps, they could take the first tentative steps towards some kind of understanding, progress beyond this antagonism.

'Before I accepted his proposal I told him I didn't love him,' she said. 'He understood that. I liked him, then, even respected him. I was grateful to him for caring for me. I was a weak fool,' she admitted dully. 'Too scared—of lots of things, but mainly of worrying Dad—to stand on my own feet. He suggested we had separate rooms because he was a light sleeper and I was pregnant and needed my rest. Nothing changed after Rosie was born. He did make one attempt to consummate the marriage.'

Her face went a dull red as she recalled the acute embarrassment of that encounter. 'It was a total failure. He'd already told me he was unable to father a child and I took it for granted that he was impotent. And I'd been about as responsive as a block of wood.' She could confess that much, but couldn't explain that, after Adam, no other man could arouse a flicker of interest in her atrophied senses.

Her voice low, her fingers laced tightly together in her lap, she continued, 'It was a relief, really. Not to have to sleep with him. But he was always kind, very considerate. I guess it paid him to be, if his grand plan was to go ahead. I seem to be,' she said, her voice bitter now, 'a hopeless judge of character.'

He could make what he liked of that statement, but all he said was, 'Thank you for your honesty. You didn't have to tell me. I have no rights where you're concerned. My rights begin and end with my daughter.'

She sensed he was about to stand up, to suggest they leave, and she felt defeated. Stupid, she thought as she followed his lead and exited the door he held open for her, but she had thought—hoped—that there had been a shift in their relationship, that he might want to spend more time talking to her.

Stupid to imagine that he, too, would feel the need for them to draw closer, to put the enmity behind them.

Following the tail-lights of his Jaguar, she made herself concentrate on her driving. Let herself think of him, his extraordinary, dog-in-the-manger admission that he hadn't been able to bear the thought of her making love with her late husband, and she would find herself driving straight into a ditch.

They were back at the cottage in time to put Rosie to bed. At the little girl's insistence, it was Adam who read her a story. Claudia went down to the kitchen and made herself a pot of tea and worried about the sleeping arrangements.

Guy slept in the narrow single room above the

stairs, Amy and Rosie in one of the two double rooms. Thankfully, both had twin beds, but she still felt edgy about sharing a room with Adam. After what had happened at his London flat, she knew he wouldn't make advances. He had clearly demonstrated his total lack of interest, which should have been a relief because if he did she wouldn't be able to resist and then where would she be? Up the creek without a paddle, fathoms-deep in love with him all over again, and letting him know it!

She still felt edgy, edgy enough to excuse herself and go to bed early, leaving the others engrossed in a TV programme she couldn't name, even though she'd had her eyes glued to the set.

Out of the bathroom in record time, she pulled one of the worn old T-shirts she wore to bed over her head, scrambled between the sheets, and, before she could switch off the bedside lamp, Adam entered.

Pain darkened her eyes. Didn't he know that the only way she could get through the night with him in a bed only a few inches away from hers was for her to pretend to be asleep when he put in an appearance? But no, of course he didn't! As far as he was concerned she was a waste of space, someone he could ignore with no trouble at all.

'I came to see if you were OK. You've been very pale all evening.'

'I'm fine.' She jerked the covers up to her chin. 'Such concern! There's no need to fake it, though. There's no one else around to be impressed.'

He narrowed his eyes then shrugged. 'If that's the way you want it.' He turned to leave and a lump of remorse settled on her chest like a heavy load of rocks. He had shown compassion when she'd been upset before, so maybe she'd misjudged him and he had been concerned.

'Adam,' she said impulsively, 'can I ask you a question?'

He turned his head, grey eyes looking long and hard into the blue of hers. She saw the rigid line of his shoulders relax a little. He almost smiled. 'I guess I owe you one.'

'About Rosie.' She knew she risked bringing his wrath back down on her head. He would never forgive her for keeping the child's existence from him. But she had to know. She had tried to puzzle it out times without number and it had been running in and out of her head all evening, ever since he'd stated that the only rights he had were those concerning his daughter. 'It's different for me. I gave birth to her, I've loved her for all of her short life. But you didn't know she existed until a few weeks ago. Yet your need to have her permanently in your life was compelling enough for you to take on my debts and marry me, even though you despise me.'

'You find that strange?' He sounded more relaxed, too. Whatever it was that had drawn his features into a tight mask at her swipe at his show of concern had gone away. He turned back into the room, shadowy with only the light from the low-wattage bedside lamp.

'I wouldn't have expected you to turn your back on her,' she explained. 'I'd have understood if you'd

wanted to see her now and then—but to saddle yourself—'

'With a mountain of debts that weren't of my making and a wife I despise,' he finished for her. He
moved back into the room and sat on the edge of her
bed. She moved her feet to accommodate him and he
said, 'I did despise you. When I learned I had a child
who was five years old I thought you were the pits.
That was before I understood what had happened,
why you'd acted the way you had. I don't condone
it, but I can't condemn.'

Did that mean he no longer despised her? She
wanted to ask, but didn't quite dare. In the dim light
his eyes looked like smoky charcoal, his mouth softer.
She wanted, oh, so badly, to kiss him.

She firmed her lips, as if that could stop her wayward thought patterns, and Adam said, 'Perhaps if I
explain why I feel the way I do about Rosie, then you
will understand, too, and stop looking on me as an
arrogant tyrant. Will that be possible, do you think?'

'Try me!' If her reply was flippant, she couldn't
help it. She could hardly say, I don't look at you that
way, I look at you and love you! Suddenly, she felt
released. She was no longer having to fight herself,
fight her feelings. She loved him, always had and
probably always would and, admitting it, could learn
to handle it.

'We both come from one-parent families, but there
the similarity ends. Tragically, you lost your mother
when you were ten and that was a dreadful thing to
happen to you, Clo.' The use of that pet name, when
there was no one around to witness it, made her heart

swell. But she hid her pleasure. He'd think her such a fool if he ever guessed how she still felt about him.

'But you had memories of happy family life, a father who loved you deeply—and dear Amy, of course. You knew why your mother had gone. My father deserted us when I was five and I didn't know why. After he went, my mother cried all the time, and pushed me away whenever I went near her. I thought it was my fault my father had left. I missed him dreadfully and kept asking when he was coming back, which only made things worse. She was bitter until the day she died.' His deep voice was soft with regrets.

Claudia's eyes stung with tears. 'Adam—I didn't know. How sad for you!'

She resolutely swallowed down the lump in her throat and he said, 'I would have been almost seven when Uncle Harold took over. He was my mother's brother, unmarried, owner of the successful Hallam Group. He later told me he'd never married because he'd got more sense than to tie himself to one woman, and to have to shell out half his fortune if said woman wanted a divorce. So, as you can perhaps imagine, he was a cold, hard, calculating man.

'My mother, he maintained, was making a mess out of bringing me up. We were to move in with him and he'd make a man out of me, fit to step into his shoes when the time came. The process involved sending me away to boarding-school. All I knew was that I didn't want to be made into a ''man'', or do anything my rather frightening uncle told me to do. I wanted my dad back.

'I can remember,' he said quickly, as if he sensed she was about to make more sympathetic noises and didn't want to have to hear them, 'the time when I told him all that—that I hated going away to school and wanted my dad back. He told me we'd never see him again. Neither did we. The last anyone heard he was in South America and that must have been a good twenty years ago. He then went on to tell me that my father had only married my mother for what he could get out of her.

'They came from a wealthy family, independent of the proceeds from the Hallam Group. My father had wanted life on easy street—flash cars, good suits, money to burn. When he finally realised that Harold—as trustee for Mother's share of the family fortune—wasn't going to play ball, he walked out.'

'That was a terrible thing to say to a small boy!' Claudia blurted, not able to stop herself. She wanted to weep, thinking about how lost, lonely and bewildered that small boy must have felt.

'Maybe,' he shrugged. 'In any case, I got over it. Settled down at school and made friends. And this is where I come to the point. Friends often invited me back for holidays and because of that I got to know what a close, loving family life was like. With two parents, both with different perspectives and life experiences—male and female—to give to their children. That's what I want for my child, for Rosie. Two parents who love her, who'll be there for her as long as she needs them. Stability, emotional security.'

'Oh, Adam!' Instinctively, she put her hand on his. She understood his motives now she knew of his background, the lack of love, the bitterness, the loss of a father who hadn't loved him enough to stay.

She had deprived him of the first five years of his daughter's life, made him—without his knowledge and against all his principles—an absent father. 'I'm so sorry!' Remorse was savage; it made tears fall unchecked. She felt his fingers tighten around hers.

'Don't,' he said. 'Don't cry, Clo.'

Which only made it worse. Sobs came and she couldn't stop them. Through the silent storm she heard him sigh, just before he moved closer and gathered her into his arms, holding her, rocking her until the sobs became shudders and died away.

It felt so wonderful to be held like this, as if she had finally come home after a long, lonely time spent in the bleak, dark wilderness of missing him. Missing his strength, his warmth, the feeling that he cared for her. But, most of all, missing his love.

He put her slightly away from him and she wanted to cry out, Don't leave me! Don't go! But he placed both hands on either side of her face, brushing the silky strands of toffee-coloured hair away from her damp cheeks, and gently kissed the last of the tears away.

The warmth of his lips branded her; she couldn't get enough of the sensation she had thought she would never experience again, and she was transported straight to heaven on a riot of breathtaking rapture and couldn't help herself when her hands pushed beneath the soft leather of his jacket.

She ran them lovingly over the fine cashmere of his sweater in ecstatic exploration and when he said, his voice sounding ragged round the edges, 'I don't think this is a good idea, Clo,' she unhesitatingly slipped her hands around his steely, tense body to his back and pulled him even closer.

The story of his childhood had touched her deeply and the remorse for what she'd done to him was hard to bear. Her emotions were all over the place and only constant was her love for him, her need. The past, what he'd done to her, no longer mattered.

She lifted her tear-stained face trustingly to his and she heard the rough intake of his breath just before he lowered his head and kissed her.

CHAPTER EIGHT

THAT kiss was like no other. Not even Claudia's explicit memories of the way it had been between them before—the explosion of sheer chemistry—lived up to the reality of this mutual, wildly passionate embrace.

She knew by the near-savage hunger of his mouth as it began to plunder hers more deeply that he was fully aware of the way her body was burning with the ravaging flames of desire, that she was desperately craving him, open to the fierce masculinity of him. He knew it and was responding to it as if he were a starving man who was being offered a banquet.

Her whole body shuddered beneath his hands as they began their fevered exploration, tremors of ecstasy, of wild sexual tension that reached deep into her heart and soul. This was her man, her love for all time, and nothing had changed. Not for her; how could it when she had been born to be his?

They had done each other deep injustices, but that was in the past. They could forget and forgive and go on to find a future together.

The sheer wonder of the thought made her want to weep again, with joy this time, but she didn't; she moaned his name aloud as he deftly removed her old T-shirt and bent his dark head to suckle her breasts.

Claudia squirmed beneath the sensual onslaught. It

was too much, yet not nearly enough; she thought she might die with the intensity of the ecstasy, the promise of more to come. And when he lowered his head, burning the soft skin of her tummy with hungry lips, she slid her hands on either side of his firm jaw and lifted his head, gazing at him with eyes limpid with love.

'Make love to me, Adam,' she murmured, her voice thick and throaty. 'Make it right.'

For a moment he went still, his eyes glittering deep into hers like hot silver knives. Her heartbeats turned hectic. Was he going to remind her that he'd said he had no intention of consummating the marriage and then walk away? Her world would fall apart if that happened!

And then his mouth curved in that wickedly sensual smile she remembered so well as she took her courage in both hands and tugged impatiently at his jacket.

Did that utterly sinful smile mean he was remembering all the eager enthusiasm for him she'd unashamedly displayed during that long, hot summer six years ago? She didn't know, and she didn't care. She was still as uninhibitedly eager for him, and only him.

Drenched in her own desire, she lay naked on the bed and watched him undress with smouldering eyes. His movements were smooth and economical, and he didn't take his eyes off hers for one second as he unbuttoned his shirt and dropped it on the floor, unzipped his jeans.

'Dear God in heaven!' he gasped raggedly when she wrapped her body around his as he slid onto the bed beside her. 'Clo!' Then he said no more, his mouth ravaging hers as her body instinctively opened to embrace his.

The dams had burst, and she surrendered willingly, easily, as if they had never been apart; surrendered to love and the driving rhythm of his body, her breathing as harsh and ragged as his. She had waited so long for this rapture, this slice of heaven that was theirs alone, waited so long for his fierce thrust of male possession, to have him fill her, body, heart and soul.

And when he finally rolled away from her he turned her in his arms and tucked her body into the curve of his, his face in her hair, his arm going around her as his hand rested intimately between her thighs.

Her head dizzy with the sheer magic of what had happened for them both, she heard his breathing almost immediately relax as he fell asleep, giving way to the weariness she'd sensed in him earlier. She gave a contented little sigh and clicked off the bedside lamp then wriggled closer, snuggling into him, careful not to disturb him.

She would not sleep. She wanted to savour every moment of this miraculous night. They were together again, in every way, and this was how it was meant to be.

When he woke they would talk. They needed to talk, to sort out the past and go on to their future. She would try to ensure that their new relationship went forward on a less tottery foundation than it had done up to now.

He most certainly didn't love her the way she loved him, but she could live with that if she had to. He wanted his daughter in his life and she understood his determination now. And he wanted her, the mother of his child, and as more than a wife in name only. He hadn't been able to hide his hunger for her.

Together, they could build a good future, give Rosie a happy, stable life with two loving parents, just the way he wanted it. And, if she was patient, he could grow to love her, too. Time and tenderness might make it happen.

Her sins would have to be confessed. She knew now that she could tell him without rancour exactly why she'd kept their child a secret from him. Surely he would understand that six years ago she had been too immature, too frightened by the threat that she might lose her father, to cope with his betrayal, to track him down, somehow, and tell him she was carrying his child because he had a right to know?

She'd taken the easy way out and had learned harsh lessons from her weakness. She couldn't condone what he had done but she could forgive. He was older, too, a fully mature adult, and he obviously had no need to look for ways—through charm and mind-blowing sex—to feather his nest.

Her brows drew together in a frown. He had never had to, had he?

She sucked in a long breath. Adam had known from a very early age that he was being groomed eventually to take over his uncle's company, plus the family wealth. Farthings Hall and her family business would have seemed very small beer by comparison!

There was no need to search her memory for what Helen had said; the words had been branded on her brain. He'd played up to her, proposed to her, because she was a considerable heiress admitting he'd messed around with her.

Now she came to think about it, really think about it, she knew Adam would never say anything like that; it was completely out of character. And he hadn't needed what Helen had said he saw as her future legacy—he had more than enough money and property of his own!

Helen had been doing what she'd been best at—lying and deceiving!

Yet during that summer he'd presented himself as a penniless drifter, content to take on the hard labour and odd jobs around the grounds to earn his keep—a pittance, and somewhere to hang his hat for a month or two.

He had never once hinted at the massive family wealth behind him. She wished he'd wake up so she could get it all clear in her head!

As if sensing her sudden restlessness he did just that, but the sensual slide of his hand up over her tummy to touch her breasts, the way he languorously turned her to him, chased every coherent thought out of her head. This time his loving was long and slow and afterwards she drifted off to sleep on a wave of exhausted contentment, and when she woke he wasn't there.

But, seconds later, Rosie was. 'Time to get up, Mummy! See—I dressed myself!'

So she had. Her sweater was inside out and her slippers were on the wrong feet. Claudia slid out of bed and into a robe and put her daughter right, gave her a kiss and a cuddle and steered her to the door. 'Tell Daddy I'll be down in a few minutes.'

She showered quickly and dressed in a pair of sleekly fitting amber-coloured cords and a cream ribbed Italian sweater she plucked out of the booty she'd brought back from London with her. She brushed her hair until it shone like shot silk and left it loose, and applied enough make-up to show she'd bothered with her appearance.

She couldn't wait for this wonderful new day to begin. The first day of the rest of her life with Adam! Quite why Helen had lied she'd probably never know. But lied she had. Adam had had no need of her future inheritance!

And a glorious day it was, too! The sun shining from a pale blue sky, hardly a breath of wind. There would be a nip in the air but that didn't matter, not if Rosie was warmly dressed. She usually planned some kind of outing with the little girl on a Saturday. Perhaps the three of them could drive to the coast, have lunch somewhere, begin the process of bonding as a loving family.

She would mention it to Adam over breakfast.

It was eight o'clock and the household was awake. Guy, always an early riser, would have been to the village stores for his preferred newspaper to read after breakfast—which was already in the making, judging by the aroma of bacon and coffee drifting up the stairwell.

Adam would be waiting for her, listening to Rosie's endless chatter, she thought happily as she practically skipped down the stairs, wondering if he'd appreciate the new-look Claudia in a sample of the perfectly fitting designer gear his generosity had enabled her to choose.

Her father and Amy were sitting over the remains of breakfast at the kitchen table and Rosie was wolfing down a bowl of cereal. No sign of Adam, no empty plate and only one unused place setting.

'Where's Adam?' Gone out for an early morning walk? She wished he'd waited; she could have gone with him, used the opportunity to ask the questions that had been pushed right out of her head late last night. As she remembered exactly why they'd been pushed out, her face went pink with pleasure. She reached out to pour herself coffee from the pot just as her father lowered his paper.

'He left at half past six, ten minutes after I came down. I expected you to be around to see him off. He'll be away some time. After all, he can't travel out to Florida on a daily basis.'

The implied criticism in her father's voice was nothing to the savage shock of knowing he'd left without saying a word to her about it. After last night she would have expected more, expected him to tell her of his planned trip, to take her in his arms and kiss her goodbye.

Her face went white and pinched and her father, obviously relenting, said gently, 'I know it must be a big disappointment—flitting hither and thither at a moment's notice, especially so soon after your marriage—but you've got enough common sense to take it in your stride. He couldn't pass up the opportunity for his company to buy into a huge leisure complex out there. That sort of thing won't happen on a regular basis.'

'And went without so much as a bite of breakfast,' Amy tutted. 'A long drive ahead of him and then goodness knows how many hours in the air, with nothing inside him!' She heaved herself out of her chair, fetched a plate out of the warming oven and put it down in front of Claudia. 'I kept yours hot for you.'

Grilled tomatoes and bacon. Claudia looked at it and felt sick, her stomach churning. Her father thought she was sulking, and her husband hadn't bothered to tell her he had a protracted business trip in the offing.

Or was it business? She drank her coffee, needing a caffeine fix, hating herself for having such a thought. What hope was there for them if she allowed such untrusting thoughts in her head? What hope when he couldn't be bothered to tell her of his movements, when he walked out without even bothering to leave her a note?

The next five weeks were a nightmare. Claudia was sure it rained every day, relentlessly, with gales sweeping in across the headlands, scouring the valleys and stripping the last of the leaves from the trees.

Having to stay indoors during out-of-school hours, Rosie grew grumpy as the days grew darker and wetter and wilder. They heard from Adam often, but there was nothing there to console Claudia in the stream of picture postcards, usually depicting Disney characters. Most of the available space was taken up with cheery messages for Rosie and his weekly phone calls were probably worse.

He'd talk to her first, and that was only for the look of it because his voice was always impersonal, clipped and cold as he briefly discussed work in progress, the new plans he'd had drawn up to higher specifications, the difficulty of finding contractors who would work to the high standard the Hallam Group demanded. All details she didn't want to know about, stuff she could relay to her interested father, nothing about how he felt, whether he was missing her, whether that magical night they had spent together had meant anything at all to him.

She wanted to ask him, to beg him to tell her why he was so distant, as if they were strangers, never lovers. But she couldn't, not while the others were in hearing distance.

And then he'd ask to speak to Rosie so she'd hand the receiver over and listen to their daughter's animated chatter and wonder, hating herself, how she could possibly be jealous of her own child. She didn't know what was happening to her.

The hardest part of all was keeping her misery to herself, making herself appear cheerful in front of the others, doing all the normal everyday things that made her want to scream and throw things at the wall. The only thing that had made her forget her inner brooding fears was when, three weeks after Adam's abrupt departure, the last of the workmen had moved out of Farthings Hall.

She'd thrown herself into the task of moving them all back as if her life had depended on it. She'd packed, ferried cases back and forth, scrubbed and polished Willow Cottage until it was as neat and shining as it had been on the day they'd taken up temporary residence.

And now, five long, painful weeks into his absence, they were home again, firmly ensconced. The builders and decorators had done a superlative job and Guy was delighted to be back in his own armchair, in his own home, with his own things around him. It was the only consolation Claudia had—seeing her father gaining so much strength, looking fitter every day. The past was behind him; he had no burdens now.

She smiled for her father across the hearth as he lowered his newspaper and wondered how long she could keep up the pretence of cheerful normality. Adam had been away for over a month and he'd made no mention of returning and, as if he'd picked up her thought waves, her father said, 'I hope Adam's home in time to go to Rosie's end-of-term school play. She's got the starring role, or so she tells me.'

Indeed she had; the little girl hadn't stopped talking about it for the last two or three days. She had made them all solemnly promise to be there to watch her and they'd cried in unison, 'Just try to stop us!' And had watched that heart-stopping smile brighten the impish little face.

So if Adam didn't show up in time she'd kill him! Because although the tiny girl hadn't had enough time to bond properly with her father Claudia knew she was proud of her brand-new daddy, looked forward to his regular postcards and weekly phone calls and was always asking when he'd come home.

He called that evening, just before Rosie's bedtime, and, aware that the little girl was hovering, her eyes big and shining, Claudia's first words were, 'Will you try to get home in time for Rosie's end-of-term play? She's got the starring role.'

Maybe she'd sounded too brusque, but her emotions were beginning to break through the tight lid she'd put on them and, her own feelings of abandonment apart, she was fiercely protective of her daughter's happiness. She was too tightly wound up to take in his response and had to ask him to repeat himself.

'I'm phoning from Heathrow. I'll be back in the small hours so don't wait up.' He sounded more remote than ever, if that was possible, but her heart skipped. Adam was coming home! They could sort out whatever it was that had caused this mental distance between them. After the long night's loving they'd shared, she was sure they could! Maybe he found it difficult to talk over the phone about anything that mattered. Maybe it was as simple as that!

'We'll talk tomorrow,' he said, as if reading her thoughts. 'And tell Rosie I wouldn't miss her play for a trillion pounds.'

'Tell her yourself.' There was a smile in her voice as she passed the receiver over and listened to the little girl's excited chatter about her part in the school play. She hugged herself, wrapping her arms around her body to contain her relief. Adam was coming home and, no matter what he'd said, she'd be waiting for him.

And she was, dressed in the most alluring of her new nightgowns—oyster satin with lots of lace—covered by the matching wrap. She bathed and perfumed herself after Guy and Amy had gone up to bed, both delighted that Adam was on his way home at last.

But nothing like as delighted as she was! And the fire was glowing in welcome, the lamplight soft, her blue eyes hazy with love and longing.

He closed the door behind him and leaned against it. He looked weary, hard lines bracketing his mouth. Wearing a dark grey business suit, he looked formidable. Claudia made herself ignore the blocks of ice that began crawling through her veins.

Of course he was tired, too tired to rake up a smile. Who wouldn't be exhausted after hours in the air and a long drive through the night? 'Welcome home,' she said, a strange catch in her voice, suddenly quite ridiculously shy.

'I told you how late I'd be. You shouldn't have waited up.'

Claudia smiled. 'Of course I should.' She stood up, saw his mouth tighten, a flinch of something that looked like pain flicker in his eyes before he looked quickly away, moved into the room and dropped his briefcase onto a table. He looked as if he'd lost weight, she thought with a protective pang, the urge to mother him surfacing for the first time, taking her by surprise.

He had always been the strong one but now he looked drained. His workload in the States must have been killing, she told herself. Maybe he'd worked extra-long hours to keep his time out there to the absolute minimum, anxious to return to his family.

The deduction gave her a rosy glow inside, thawing away the trickle of ice produced by his cold greeting. 'Sit by the fire and relax,' she said lightly. 'You need looking after. I know we've got lots to talk about, but that can wait until you've slept.' Apart from anything else, she had such wonderful news to tell him, but even that could wait. Right now he needed cherishing. 'I made sandwiches—roast beef and horseradish— your favourite! I'll fetch them. Would you like a hot drink, or would whisky go down better?'

'Forget the food. I don't want it.' He was already pouring whisky from the decanter. He tilted it in her direction, one dark brow raised, and Claudia shook her head, her mouth trembling. He was shutting her out. Something bad had happened since the night they'd made love.

'Since you chose to wait up, and the rest of the household is sensibly asleep, we may as well have that talk now. At least we won't be interrupted.'

His voice was flat, his words ominous. Claudia's bones turned to water. She stepped back shakily, feeling for the edge of the chair with the back of her legs, and sank down, watching him move to the fire, looking into the flames, his head bowed.

'Adam?' Somehow she found her voice, but it was a poor, thin thing. He turned and looked at her then, his eyes bleak, and in that moment she knew that whatever chance they might have had had gone.

'Right.' He dragged in a breath. He stood straight again, six feet something of hard male purpose. 'We might as well get it over and done with. It's quite simple. I made a mistake. Marrying you was the biggest mistake of my life and I apologise for it. It won't work. So I suggest we go for a two-year separation and then a divorce. We'll keep it amicable, for Guy and Rosie's sake. Naturally, I'll continue to support you all and I'll want to see my daughter regularly— her school play, for instance. Apart from that, we'll arrange access to suit you.'

A log fell in the hearth, sending a shower of sparks up the wide chimney. Claudia flinched, the small, everyday sound startling her. She couldn't get her head round what he was saying.

'You said you wanted your daughter to have two parents around—you even told me why.' She pushed the words out with difficulty. When he'd insisted on marriage that had been the overriding reason, so important to him that he'd taken on a wife he despised, shouldered the burden of her debts.

Yet now, when he'd heard her story and changed his mind about despising her, when he'd demonstrated just how much he still wanted her physically, he was calling it a day, walking out on them all. Savaging her heart all over again.

'It was a mistake,' he said again. 'You knew that before I did. You did everything you could to wriggle out of that commitment to begin with. I should have listened. Stubbornly, I did not.' He drained his glass, made a grimace of distaste—not at the whisky, she guessed, but at the situation he found himself in.

'Fortunately, no damage can have been done as far as Rosie's concerned. I've only been in her life for a very short time and not on anything like a permanent basis. I don't applaud it, but these days divorce is commonplace. Provided it's amicable and the child has regular access to the absent parent, then the damage can be limited. Especially in Rosie's case—she's never been used to having me around.'

Pain, bitterness, it was all there. Was he unable to forgive her for keeping his daughter's existence from him? Maybe if she explained just why she had it would help?

'Can't we discuss this?'

'There's nothing to discuss. The marriage won't work. I'm ending it.'

Just like that!

Her feelings didn't matter. Had they ever mattered to him? Did what he want always take precedence, even over his daughter? Didn't he care what havoc he left in his careless wake? Anger and outrage pulsed through her, making her shake with the intensity of it.

She stood up, her face white and tight with fury. 'Adam.' Her voice was low, a warning growl, warning of storms about to break. He turned away from her, pouring himself another inch of whisky.

'I'm not getting into a slanging match with you, Claudia. Just go to bed.'

The cold and expert dismissal drained the fight right out of her.

After a shocked pause she stumbled from the room, utterly diminished.

CHAPTER NINE

THE gale woke her before the alarm clock did. Claudia went through the early morning ritual of getting Rosie washed and dressed, ready for school, then put herself into old jeans and a thick woolly sweater. She did everything numbly, still in shock. She still couldn't believe that Adam had so coldly and finally ended their marriage. She could hardly take it in.

She didn't know where he'd slept; it certainly hadn't been with her in the sumptuous master suite she'd earmarked for their use. If she hadn't felt so numb she would probably have been crying her eyes out, she thought as she boiled Rosie's breakfast egg and made toast soldiers. At least she had something to be grateful for.

Amy and Guy were full of Adam's return, wanting to know what time he'd finally arrived, if he was going to stay put this time and do most of his work from home, as he'd said he would. For the first time in her life she wished the two of them, so very dear to her, a million miles away.

She fielded the questions as best she could, wondering how she would be able to break the news of the marriage breakdown, sounding regretful but adult about it, explaining that they'd both decided, amicably, that it would never work. She would probably break down completely, fall into a million miserable

pieces. These two loving souls didn't deserve to have
to share a burden of misery that was hers alone.

'I suppose he's still out for the count.' Guy smiled
comfortably and Claudia mumbled something and
helped Rosie into her school uniform coat, popping
her beret on her soft dark hair and hooking her school
bag over her tiny shoulders. It was almost as big as
she was and at this point Claudia always grinned because who wouldn't? The little girl looked so cute.

But not this morning. Her face felt like a block of
wood.

'Not out for the count but up and running,' Adam
answered his father-in-law's comment from the doorway. Claudia's heart jolted painfully. The sight of him
had pulled her back into the land of the living.

He looked as gorgeous as ever. Freshly showered,
dressed in a slick waterproof over black sweater and
jeans, there was no sign of the bleak weariness of the
night before. Claudia could hardly credit that the
scene between them had ever happened. Every time
she saw him she loved him more and she mourned
the loss of the numbness that had helped her through
this morning because now she was stinging with pain
all over again.

'I'll do the school run,' he offered, his silver eyes
heartbreakingly soft as he smiled down at his diminutive offspring. But a muscle was jerking spasmodi-
cally at the side of his jaw so, try as he might to hide
it, he was under strain, too.

Claudia said thickly, 'There's really no need.'

'Wait with her in the hall while I bring the car right
up to the door; it's pouring with rain.' He spoke as if

she hadn't said a thing. He lobbed a smile in the direction of the kitchen table. 'See you guys later.' Then he took hold of Rosie's hand and headed out.

When the Jaguar was parked he carried Rosie out and strapped her into the passenger seat. The little girl's face was bright with the excitement of having her daddy back and driving her to school, and Claudia could have wept her heart out.

He was back to where she was standing in the shelter of the doorway in seconds, raindrops glistening on the shoulders of his waterproof, spangling his hair. 'I suggest you break the news to Guy and Amy while I'm out.' There was nothing in his eyes to tell her what he was thinking, nothing but an endless blankness.

'Coward!' She spat the word out. His final words last night had stunned her but the numbness had gone now and all the anger and pain came blistering back.

He ignored the taunt, his tone as level and dry as a desert plain. 'It would be better if you quietly prepared the ground. I'll be back later to speak to them myself. I'll be leaving after that, but I'll keep in touch. I'll need to know the date and time of Rosie's play; I have no intention of missing that. We'll sort out a reasonable access agreement later.'

Claudia closed the door in his face and paced the floor, trying to get her rioting emotions under control. She wanted to hit him, oh, how she wanted to hit him!

Everything was for his own convenience. He decided something and it suddenly became immutable law! So he could sit twiddling his thumbs until his beard grew long and white because she sure as hell wasn't going to do a single thing he'd told her to!

Far from carrying out orders, she shot upstairs and made Rosie's bed and then her own, then stood staring out at the rain. The wind was blowing the trees into twisted shapes and Old Ron would be drinking his morning tea and muttering about the weather and Bill would probably be working in the glasshouses.

She didn't know why she'd been standing there, staring out, until the Jaguar purred to a halt on the drive. Adam was back. Unconsciously she'd been waiting for him. Her heart thumped painfully against her ribs. He would enter the house, expecting her to have 'prepared the ground', and find himself uttering platitudes to people who didn't know what he was talking about. Then he would have to explain, do his own dirty work!

But he turned away from the house, pulled up the collar of his waterproof and strode off, heading across the sodden lawns. There was only one place he would be going to from that direction and Claudia knew where that was.

She dragged a new, bright yellow padded jacket from the hanging cupboard, stuffed her feet into boots and headed after him. There was something she needed to tell him in private, and the cove in this weather was as private as it got.

If it was the last thing she did on this earth, she would make him listen, and he needn't think he could issue orders and then walk away, end their marriage, deprive his child of the permanent father he'd been so adamant that she needed.

How dared he do that to them without a single word of explanation? Saying it wouldn't work wasn't good enough. And why wouldn't it work? He hadn't told her. She would demand a proper explanation; he owed her that much!

The rain had eased considerably but the wind was a savage monster, rampaging up the narrow valley, making headway almost impossible.

As her feet finally hit sand she paused to snatch her breath back, her chest heaving as she dragged the sharp air into her tortured lungs.

Adam was standing near the edge of the crashing waves; she could hardly see him through the wildly tossing spray. The sound of the wind and water in turmoil was deafening.

He didn't see her or hear her until she touched his arm. His eyes narrowed against the onslaught of the gale, he looked down at her, his mouth tight.

Claudia opened her own mouth to let her anger and frustration pour out but shut it again because she knew he wouldn't hear a word she said above the noisy violence of the storm. She shouldn't have come, she thought, sinking back into the misery of despair. It had been a stupid idea. She should have waited for his eventual return and tackled him then.

As always, he seemed able to pluck her tumbling thoughts right out of her mind. He shrugged as if bowing to the inevitable then took her arm, helping her over the sand, farther up into the cove where the rocky outcrop of the sheltering cliffs gave some respite from the ceaseless buffeting of the wild wind.

'What do you want?' He released her immediately,

as if he couldn't bear to touch her, and pushed his wet dark hair back from his forehead with his fingers. She felt the fight, the painful anger drain from her.

A confrontational attitude would get her nowhere with this man. He would simply close down, shut her out. In any case, she no longer wanted to lash out at him, to try to punish him for his cold infliction of pain. She wanted to hold him, tell him how very much she loved him.

But wanting a thing didn't make it happen. She would have to find the courage to make such an admission, lay herself open to his scorn or disbelief or, perhaps worst of all, his indifference.

She raised troubled eyes to his. 'What brought you here, in this weather?' She had expected him to arrive back at the house, collect his few belongings, say his goodbyes and move out of her life.

'I wanted to say goodbye to my memories,' he answered tersely. 'Satisfied?'

Memories of the first time they'd made love? Of the time they'd laughed at the fury of that long-ago summer storm? Or the much more recent Indian summer picnic when he'd taken the first steps towards bonding with his daughter?

The latter, she guessed, not daring to ask.

She shivered, the chill of her flesh beneath her rain-sodden clothes making itself known. Adam said flatly, 'Get back to the house before you catch pneumonia.'

She wasn't going anywhere without him. She backed further into the shelter of the rocks and saw his eyes darken, as stormy as the elements that raged around them. It was, she knew, now or never. Her stomach clenched with tension and she had to force the words out.

'You've made up your mind to divorce me. I don't understand why, but I accept it because I've got no option. But I want you to know that I love you. I never stopped loving you.'

'Liar,' he came back dismissively. 'What sort of love rejects the father of an unborn child in favour of a man who is seen as a better provider?' His mouth was a hard, compressed line, the words snapped out through his teeth. 'I'm heading back; you can do as you damn well please!'

She caught him before he'd reached the open beach, dragging on his arm to hold him back. She would not take that accusation, not from anyone, not from him. 'Don't call me a liar! You did nothing but lie to me when we first met!'

He was staring straight ahead, not looking at her, not dignifying her accusation with a reply. But when she grated, 'You lived a lie. You pretended you were a penniless drifter and all the time you had a fortune behind you,' she watched the furious jerk of a muscle at the side of his hard jaw and knew her words had hit their target.

He turned and looked at her, bitterness in his eyes, his voice bleakly sarcastic. 'Now why would I do that, I wonder?' Then emotion powered its way through, making him sound tough, aggressive. 'I've been hounded by women on the make since I reached my late teens. Not for myself, but for the background wealth, because of who I was destined to become— the head of the Hallam Group. It was a hard lesson to have to learn, but believe me I learned it quickly and well. That summer I wanted time out to be myself. Since I was seven years old my uncle had mapped my life out for me; I'd just finished my degree course in architecture and land use studies and I wanted to bum around all summer, picking up the odd temporary job, taking time out before having to knuckle down to running the Group. And what happened?'

His mouth curled bitterly. 'I met you. I fell in love with you. I had never known such happiness. You loved me back, or so you said. Loved me for myself, not the Hallam wealth. You promised to marry me. I knew I'd have to tell you the truth about myself, but you got there first. Told me it was over, you were seeing someone else, someone with a proper job and money in the bank. You were worse than the others. You were carrying my child.' His eyes stabbed her. 'Now tell me you never stopped loving me!'

'But I didn't!' she cried. In view of what he'd just told her, the way she'd broken things off between them six years ago, she knew she had little hope of convincing him. 'I love you, penniless or not. I didn't know I was pregnant until you'd gone. I had no means of finding you. And to be honest—' she almost faltered there, but she had to be completely truthful because the need for honesty was all that was left between them now '—at that time I didn't want to.'

'So you married Favel.' His tone was an indictment. In his eyes she'd been tried, judged and convicted.

'I've already told you why.' The storm was dying

now but her voice barely carried. She injected more strength into it and told him firmly, 'The only thing I haven't told you is why I broke it off between us.'

'Now there's a thought,' he said dryly. 'Perhaps you didn't like the colour of my eyes or thought my feet a touch too big!'

'Don't!' Her eyes pleaded with him, huge blue pools in her small pale face. 'That day, I saw you storm out of Helen's bedroom—' She almost lost it there, so deeply ashamed of her younger, weaker self, but forced herself on, to lay her sins at his feet. 'She told me you'd tried to seduce her, knowing Guy was out of the way. That you'd said you'd been messing about with me because you wanted to marry money, but you wanted her.'

'And you believed her!' His eyes sharpened to pinpricks of silver, total disgust written on his hard, unforgiving features.

'At the time, yes. She was everything I wasn't— slender, perfectly groomed, beautiful,' she confessed miserably. 'I saw no reason for her to lie about a thing like that. I didn't know what she was capable of then. We'd always got on well; I never dreamed she'd lie like that; why should I? But I've thought about it since—since we met up again and I knew what Helen and Tony had been like. Liars, both of them. Cheats. I don't believe a word of what she told me now.'

He stared at her. 'How big of you! Just for the record, she'd been giving me the come-on ever since Guy gave me that temporary job—in between disappearing for hours on end with the man you decided you wanted to marry. It sickened me! And on the day you're talking about—which was probably the worst day I've lived through—she asked me to go to her room to fix a curtain pole that was coming adrift.'

His mouth twisted sardonically. 'And wouldn't you know it, she was waiting, wearing next to nothing, offering a little of what she called "adult fun", something she was sure I wasn't getting from her teenage stepdaughter. She'd noticed the amount of time we were spending together and couldn't see what I saw in what she called "that naive lump"—unless it was her future inheritance.

'I saw red, called her a few unrepeatable names and, as you so aptly put it, stormed out, leaving her telling me to get off the property. Fast. I'd already suspected something was going on between her and Favel and I couldn't stand the thought of a decent, honourable man like your father being tied to such a creature. Of course I was angry! And your so-called love for me wasn't strong enough to let you come to me and ask for my side of the story.' The harsh lines of his mouth castigated her. 'You didn't trust me. You believed what that woman said. You sure as hell didn't give me a hearing.'

'I'm sorry.' It wasn't enough to repair the damage, but what else could she say? She bowed her head. She deserved everything he said to her. 'I don't have much defence, if any. But remember I was just out of school, naive as they come. I didn't have a cynical bone in my body; I believed Helen was in love with my father; I had no reason to think she'd lie. I just didn't think people acted like that. I was young, desperately hurt, but I had some pride. I wasn't going to snivel and grovel in front of you and I wanted to hurt you back. I didn't know, then, that the last thing you needed to do was marry for money. And anyway—' there was a rough edge to her voice now; some of the blame had to be his '—you spent quite a time, when we first met, asking me about the property, what it felt like to know that I'd inherit the lot.'

'So I did.' His eyes were unforgiving, unmoved by her feeble defence. 'We were in similar positions. I wanted to know if you felt—as I was inclined to feel in those days—that duty to family expectations and the management of a large inheritance wasn't all a bed of roses.'

He lost all interest, his eyes scanning the clouds as they scudded overhead. The rain had all but stopped and the wind was dropping. He said, finality stamped on his features, 'Your pride was stronger than your love. You didn't trust me. That's the bottom line. I don't think there's any more that can be usefully said, do you? Coming?'

She followed him across the wet sand, her heart as leaden as her legs. She had tried and had failed; there was no way she could get through to him.

He helped her over the rougher patches on the path up through the valley but there was no verbal contact. He'd shut off from her, effectively cutting her out of his life. She was yesterday's woman with a vengeance.

She felt too awful to do anything but accept it now and when they met Bill, barrowing a load of logs to the fuel store, she just stared at him blankly as if she didn't know who he was.

'You two been for a swim!' He eyed their sodden clothing with a grimace. 'Clearing up now, though. Oh, Amy couldn't find you, Mrs Weston. She said, if I saw you, to tell you as Mr Sullivan's driven her to the shops.' He grinned up at Adam. 'Something about a welcome-home dinner!'

He trundled his load away and Adam hustled her in through the door to the kitchen quarters. She wished he'd go now, just leave. Leave her to come to terms with a future without him. When he was around she just couldn't think straight. Perhaps she had never been able to. She certainly hadn't been thinking straight when Helen had told those lies.

She shivered in reaction to the warmth of the kitchen and Adam said roughly. 'Look, if it's any consolation, I was guilty, too.' He had shucked off his waterproof and was pulling off her soaked jacket. She couldn't think why he was bothering, not when he couldn't wait to get away.

'Thinking about it, it was hurt pride that kept me from refusing to accept what you'd said. I just went. And never came back. Before that day I'd believed I knew you, everything about you—you were always so open and giving. I should have known you weren't capable of being so mercenary.

'Pride sent me away and kept me away. I can understand now why you acted the way you did. And I accept an equal part of the blame. But pride didn't stop me loving you, wanting you, remembering. I looked at other women and only saw you. When I twisted your arm to make you marry me I was punishing myself. When I heard that the Hall was on the market I was compelled to come back. I thought you and your father and that bitch Helen were long gone. I thought I could find out what had happened to you. So I guess we're about quits.'

He was frowning at the wet patches on her sweater where the rain had soaked through her coat, at the way her sodden jeans clung uncomfortably to her legs. Claudia's mouth dropped open as she tried to make sense of what he'd just said. She stared at him, frowning, as he said briskly, 'You need to get those wet things off and have a hot bath.'

Common sense. But if she did that he'd be gone by the time she'd finished. Wouldn't he? She shook her head and gasped as the room swam round. 'I want—'

'A hot bath,' he stated firmly. 'You're on the point of collapse.'

He carried her up the stairs that led directly from the kitchen and she let him, winding her arms around his neck, clinging on weakly. Could he possibly have meant that he'd loved her for all this time, as she had loved him, deep in her heart?

Had she done or said something since their marriage to convince him that it wouldn't work?

He pushed at the door to one of the suites with his foot. So this was where he'd slept last night. His open suitcase was on the floor, the suit he'd arrived in flung all anyhow over the back of one of the chairs.

Marching through to the *en suite* bathroom, he propped her like a doll against the washbasin and bent to run hot water into the bath.

She said to his back, 'What happened to make you

think our marriage wouldn't work, that not even Rosie was worth staying on for?'

He swung round, straightening. He said thickly, 'You know what happened. We made love. When I proposed marriage with a non-consummation pact, I believed I could hack it, for Rosie's sake. I knew that if I ever gave in to the temptation to touch you I'd be putting myself through the emotional mill again. You'd had me on the rack before; I wasn't going to put myself there again—but I wanted our child to have two parents. Why do you think I cut our so-called honeymoon short? Because I wanted to make it a real one. I held you in my arms and wanted you like hell.

'So I dumped you back at the cottage and took off. I put my lawyers to work on tracking down the embezzled money—they traced it to a Swiss account and I heard yesterday that they've managed to release it through a court order. It's yours, by the way—your independence. Then, for the rest of that first time away, all I did was try to get my head straight. I didn't dare make our marriage a real one. I came back and look what happened—I took you to bed. It was the worst thing I could have done under the circumstances as I saw them then. I was laying myself open to the Lord alone knew how much hurt at the hands of the woman who'd kept my child from me, who had vowed she loved me in one breath then swanned off to marry a man with better prospects. So I removed myself from temptation and decided to call it a day. I couldn't handle it.'

He began to strip off her wet clothes and she saw how his hands shook. Her heart took wings.

'My brain's gone silly,' she whispered. 'Are you telling me you still want me as much as ever?' And dared she say it? 'That you still love me?'

He had stripped off the last wisp of underwear, and his eyes were smoky. 'I'll tell you if you promise that what you said while I was covering myself with drama down on the beach was true.'

'That I love you, that I never stopped?' She looked up at him with love-drenched eyes, her lashes wet with unshed tears. 'I swear it on our daughter's life!'

'That's got to be good enough for me!' His voice was gruff as he scooped her up and put her in the warm water. 'I love you, probably more than you'll ever know, and I don't intend to lose you to a chill, or worse.' He smiled at her through the haze of steam, that wonderful, bone-melting smile that never failed to make her lose her head.

But his eyes were moist with emotion as he touched her wet hair. 'Let's make this day the beginning of our marriage, keep this anniversary as our special secret.'

The radiance of her smile lit up the room. She held up her arms to him. 'I'm not the only one in danger of catching a chill. Why don't you join me? The water's lovely.'

Adam needed no second invitation. And when he slipped in behind her he stretched his legs along the length of hers, his hands taking the place of the scented water that lapped her breasts.

Claudia wriggled back ecstatically into his body, a

whole future of loving this man stretching enticingly before her. She turned her head to kiss the side of his jaw and whispered, 'I've got something to tell you.'

'I don't want to know.' His deep voice was tender, threaded with amusement. 'Talking's the last thing on my mind.'

'So I gather!' The extent of his arousal was impossible to ignore. Ignoring it was the last thing on *her* mind. But she said, 'Yes, you do. Want to know, that is.' Her words ended on a gasp as he began to nuzzle her neck. 'I'll set you a riddle.'

He groaned. His mouth moved along the damp skin of her shoulder, his hands stroking her breasts. His groan was more visceral; his brain was reluctant to engage in guessing games.

'What happens when two people get carried away on a tide of unstoppable passion?' she asked huskily. Her whole body was on fire now, burning beneath his caresses.

She'd turned her head to him and he leaned forward to take her lips, teasing them, his tongue playing with hers. 'This?' he asked throatily.

'No, no, no! Pay attention!' She tried to sound like a schoolmarm and failed. A giggle built up inside her. 'They don't stop to think of precautions. They just get carried away. At least, I don't know about anyone else, but that's what seems to happen to us.'

He went very still. She leaned back against him, no longer afraid of his reaction. Not even when he exited the bath in a shower of water, scooped her out and wrapped her in a huge, fluffy towel.

He carried her to the bed and laid her down, sitting

close to her, his eyes holding hers intently. 'Another baby?'

She nodded. His silver eyes were suspiciously bright. Tears or bath water? She levered herself up and tasted the moisture with her tongue. It was salt.

'Clo, my dearest love. You waited up for me last night to tell me.' He sounded in no doubt about the truth of that. 'And all I could do was give you a verbal thrashing.'

'Don't!' She reached out and drew him down onto the bed beside her. This was a happy time. The happiest. 'No more looking back,' she whispered against his mouth. 'Only forward.'

'Only forward,' he agreed, and sweetly deepened the kiss.

The welcome-home dinner was a huge success. Claudia felt as if she was wrapped in warmth and roses, never far from her husband's side, their eyes meeting, silently speaking to each other of deeply passionate love and tender devotion.

Rosie had been allowed to stay up. Claudia had put her in her very best dress, then picked out a pair of honey-gold, silky-soft trousers, matching jacket and cream-coloured camisole for herself.

She felt beautiful for the first time in her life, and by the way Adam looked at her she knew she wasn't kidding herself.

Amy had excelled herself and when they'd finished the first course Claudia insisted, 'Stay right where you are; you've done enough, Amy. I'll clear the dishes and bring in the pud.'

'It's only one of my trifles.' The housekeeper made it sound like nothing to get excited over, but her face was pink with pride at the compliments her beef Wellington and tender vegetables had earned her.

Guy insisted on helping her and while she was stacking the used dishes in the dishwasher he said, 'So, finally, everything's all right between you two.'

Claudia's face went pink. Could he tell that she and Adam had spent most of the afternoon in bed together? Her back still firmly turned, she asked, her attempt at lightness ruined by a husky delivery, 'What are you trying to say?'

'I tried not to let it show, but you two had me worried for a while.' His voice was amused but laced with deep affection. 'Seeing you together, six years ago, I knew you were meant for each other. Then Adam disappeared and you married Tony. I knew Rosie was Adam's child—the likeness was remarkable—and when he reappeared and dropped his marriage bombshell I guessed it was for the sake of the child and prayed you'd eventually get it together again.'

She straightened then, facing him. She should have remembered how perceptive her father was where her interests were concerned. About to reassure him, he did the job himself, his eyes twinkling at her. 'My prayers were answered. That air of invincible togetherness is back again. Come here.'

She went into his open arms and returned his hug. She couldn't speak for a long, emotional moment. She was surrounded by love and warmth and so much happiness. Her heart swelled to contain her huge joy and she managed throatily, 'Better carry the trifle through before Rosie expires from thwarted expectation!'

Together, she and Adam finally put their sleepy daughter to bed then walked down the great staircase, hand in hand.

'Shall we tell them the news about the new baby tonight, Clo? Or would you rather wait until it's confirmed, until you're quite sure?'

'Oh, I'm sure.' She grinned up at him. 'Would I have told you if I hadn't been?' She tugged at his hand. 'Let's tell them. Amy will have the coffee ready by now, and if I know Dad he'll unearth a bottle of champagne from somewhere!'

She was right on both counts, correct in assuming they'd be as delighted as she and Adam were. Adam touched his foaming glass to the modest inch in hers—a concession to her condition—and said, his eyes smiling into hers, 'From now on I'm the complete family man. What I can't handle from home will be delegated. I'm going to be changing nappies and wiping bibs well into the distant future!'

His secret meaning, just for the two of them, made her melt with happiness. This was her man, her love, and their future was only just beginning.

Take 2 bestselling love stories FREE

Plus get a FREE surprise gift!

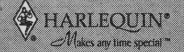

For a limited time, Harlequin and Silhouette have an offer you just can't refuse.

In November and December 1998:

BUY **ANY** TWO HARLEQUIN
OR SILHOUETTE BOOKS and
SAVE $10.00
off future purchases

OR BUY ANY THREE HARLEQUIN OR SILHOUETTE BOOKS
AND **SAVE $20.00** OFF FUTURE PURCHASES!

(each coupon is good for $1.00 off the purchase of two
Harlequin or Silhouette books)

JUST BUY 2 HARLEQUIN OR SILHOUETTE BOOKS, SEND US YOUR
NAME, ADDRESS AND 2 PROOFS OF PURCHASE (CASH REGISTER
RECEIPTS) AND HARLEQUIN WILL SEND YOU A COUPON BOOKLET
WORTH $10.00 OFF FUTURE PURCHASES OF HARLEQUIN OR
SILHOUETTE BOOKS IN 1999. SEND US 3 PROOFS OF PURCHASE AND
WE WILL SEND YOU 2 COUPON BOOKLETS WITH A TOTAL SAVING OF
$20.00. (ALLOW 4-6 WEEKS DELIVERY) OFFER EXPIRES
DECEMBER 31, 1998.

I accept your offer! Please send me a coupon booklet(s), to:

NAME: _____

ADDRESS: _____

CITY: _____ STATE/PROV.: _____ POSTAL/ZIP CODE: _____

Send your name and address, along with your cash register
receipts for proofs of purchase, to:

In the U.S.	In Canada
Harlequin Books	Harlequin Books
P.O. Box 9057	P.O. Box 622
Buffalo, NY	Fort Erie, Ontario
14269	L2A 5X3

PHQ4982

Coming Next Month

HARLEQUIN PRESENTS®

THE BEST HAS JUST GOTTEN BETTER!